THE SILENCE

OF THE WAVE

Gianrico Carofiglio

Translated by Howard Curtis

BITTER LEMON PRESS
LONDON

BITTER LEMON PRESS

First published in the United Kingdom in 2013 by
Bitter Lemon Press, 37 Arundel Gardens, London W11 2LW

www.bitterlemonpress.com

First published in Italian as *Il silenzio dell'onda*
by Rizzoli – RCS Libri S.p.A., Milan, 2011

© Gianrico Carofiglio, 2011
English translation © Howard Curtis, 2013

This edition published by arrangement with
Rosaria Carpinelli Consulenze Editoriali srl.

A CIP record for this book is available from the British Library

ISBN 978–1–908524–23–2

Typeset by Tetragon, London
Printed and bound by CPI Group (UK) Ltd, Croydon, CR0 4YY

The Silence of the Wave

1

For the third time he passed her outside the doctor's front door. It was on a Monday, at the same hour as usual. But he was certain he had seen her somewhere even before these encounters, although he had no idea where or when.

Maybe she was also a patient and had an appointment at four, he said to himself as he climbed the stairs to the doctor's office.

He rang the bell. After a moment or two the door opened, and the doctor let him in. As usual, they walked in silence down the corridor, between shelves filled with books, came to the office and sat down, Roberto in front of the desk, the doctor behind it.

"So, how are things today? Last time you were in a bad mood."

"I'm better today. I don't know why, but as I was coming up the stairs, I remembered an old story from my first years in the Carabinieri."

"Tell me."

"After finishing the officers' training academy, I was posted as a sergeant to a station in a small town in Milan province."

"Was that normal for a first posting?"

"Oh, yes, perfectly normal. It was a quiet place. Too quiet in fact; nothing ever happened. The commanding officer – an elderly marshal – was a peaceable character who always liked to sort things out in a good-natured way. I don't think he even liked arresting people. Not that there were many arrests anyway. A few petty crooks, a few small-time drug dealers at most."

"How about you?"

"I'm sorry?"

"Did you like arresting people?"

Roberto hesitated for a moment.

"Put like that, it doesn't sound very good, I guess, but yes, I did. A real law-enforcement officer – and not all carabinieri, not all policeman are – lives for arrests. From a professional point of view, I mean. If you do your work well, in the end you want to see the result, and there's no point in denying that the result you're looking for is someone ending up behind bars."

Roberto thought a moment longer about what he had just said. It was something he'd always taken for granted but, formulated as a coherent thought and uttered out loud, it acquired an unexpected, even unpleasant significance. He shook his head, and made an effort to get back to his story.

"One day I'm at the barber's when I hear shouts from the street, and I look out and see a woman running, dragging a child after her. I stand up and remove my towel. The barber's really alarmed and tells me not to do anything stupid. But we're in the North, I think to myself, why's he telling me that? Things like this happen in the South. I tell him I'm a carabiniere, though he already knows that, and then I run out and catch up with the woman."

"What had happened?"

"There was a bank robbery in progress, about a hundred yards away."

"I see."

"I remember everything very well. I took out my pistol, slid the rack back to load it, lowered the hammer to avoid a shot going off accidentally, and moved. When I got to the corner, just before the entrance to the bank, I noticed a Volvo with its engine on, but nobody inside."

"It was outside the bank?"

"No, it was round the corner. About thirty yards from the entrance, but in a side street. The bank was on the high street. I got in, switched off the engine and took the keys."

"But why had they left the car unattended?"

"The two who had gone into the bank were taking their time, and the driver had gone in to tell them to hurry up. Obviously, we only found that out later. I'd just turned the corner when I saw them all come out. I tried to remember what they'd told us in training about what to do in such a situation."

"What had they told you?"

"Not to do anything stupid. If there was a robbery, we had to call for back-up and keep an eye on the situation, but avoid going in on our own."

"So the barber wasn't wrong."

"That's true."

"And then?"

"At that particular moment, I forgot all about what I'd been taught."

"They were armed, obviously?"

"Two guns. When I saw them come out I shouted 'Halt! Carabinieri!' I remembered that because I'd repeated it so many times to myself, waiting for the first opportunity to arise."

It struck Roberto that he had almost never told this story before, and he had the feeling that behind this one memory were a whole heap of others. For a few moments he felt overwhelmed, and couldn't continue. He didn't think he could tell any story at all, because he'd be unable to choose which one to tell.

"So you said, 'Halt! Carabinieri!' And then what happened?"

The doctor's voice set the stalled mechanism back in motion.

"In their report, my superiors wrote that the robbers opened fire and Sergeant Roberto Marías responded with his service pistol. But I don't really know who fired first. All I know is that a few seconds later, one of them was on the ground, in front of the entrance to the bank, and the other two were running away. What happened immediately after that is the part I remember best. I knelt down, took aim and fired off a full magazine of bullets."

Roberto told the rest of the story. A second robber went down, hit in the leg. The third was stopped later. The one shot in front of the bank was seriously wounded but pulled through. A few days after the shoot-out Roberto was summoned by the commander of the criminal investigations unit, who congratulated him, told him he would certainly be decorated, and asked him if he would like to be transferred to Milan. Roberto accepted, and that was how, at not even twenty-three, he found himself doing the job for which he had joined the Carabinieri: detective.

"So that's how it all started?" the doctor said.

"That's how it all started."

"And you say this story came back into your mind as you were climbing the stairs to come here?"

"That's right."

"And before that you'd been thinking of something else to tell me about?"

"Yes. I wanted to tell you about a dream I had last night."

"What did you dream about?"

"Surfing. I dreamed I was on the waves."

"Surfing? Is that a sport you've ever practised?"

Roberto was silent for a while, seeing remote, silent waves and thinking about how pungent the ocean smelled, although he couldn't bring the smell back.

"I surfed when I was a boy, before I came to Italy with my mother."

He was about to continue but then either couldn't find the words or the memories, or else couldn't summon up the courage. So he remained silent and avoided looking at the doctor, who waited a couple of minutes and then said that would be enough for this afternoon.

"See you next Thursday."

Roberto looked at him, waiting for him to add something. It always seemed as if he had something to add, but he never did. See you next Monday. See you next Thursday. And that was it. Roberto would leave the office with a vague sense of frustration, although lately that had been combined with a touch of relief.

* * *

Life had started to take on a semblance of order after so many months of drifting.

He was even managing to sleep. With the help of drops, of course, but nothing in comparison with a few months earlier, when he'd had to take really powerful pills that would plunge him into a deep, leaden sleep.

He'd also started to do a bit of exercise, every now and again he tried to read the newspaper, he had almost stopped drinking, and he'd cut his cigarette consumption down to less than ten a day.

And then there were the walks.

The doctor had suggested he go for long walks. So long that he got back home tired, or rather, exhausted. He had been quite sceptical at first, but he'd gone along with it, the way you go along with a medical prescription – what else was this, after all? – and almost immediately had realized, to his surprise, that for one reason or another the walks worked.

11

He would concentrate on his steps, mentally repeating the sequence. Heel, sole, push, move. And again heel, sole, push, move. Ad infinitum, like a mantra.

This new-found awareness had a hypnotic effect and helped to drain away his bad moods. Sometimes Roberto would walk up to three or four hours non-stop, and it seemed quite healthy to feel tired at the end. It was nothing like the exhaustion and confusion of the previous few months.

It wasn't that he didn't think about anything during these walks. That, of course, would have been the best thing. But the speed and the concentration on movement stopped the thoughts from lingering too long in his head. All kinds of things would come into his mind, but they would immediately slip away to be replaced by others.

The days and weeks had taken on a rhythm. The week gravitated around his two appointments with the doctor, on Monday and Thursday. The day revolved around his endless, hypnotic walking.

Occasionally, one of his colleagues would phone him and ask him if he'd like to go out for a coffee or maybe a pizza. At first he'd always refused politely, but they would insist and after a while he'd realized that it was less of a bother to accept the invitation. He would humour his colleague's attentive if guarded attitude towards him and wait for the moment when he would be able to say goodbye and leave. Sometimes he would feel as if he were hanging over an abyss. But then he would return home and listen to the stereo or watch TV until it was time to take his drugs and fall into a chemical sleep.

Giacomo

I saw my father last night. When you put it like that, it doesn't sound so strange – seeing your father – even if it was at night.

But the thing is, he's dead.

Four years ago, he left home after an argument with Mum and never came back. It wasn't until much later that they told me he was dead. I was seven and a half.

This was the first time I'd dreamed about him since he went away. In the dream he was smiling – he didn't often smile – and for some reason it reminded me of the time he took me to the zoo for my seventh birthday, the last one we spent together.

I met my father on a tree-lined avenue in the middle of a beautiful park full of lawns and woods. He came towards me and held out his hand, as if introducing himself. I thought that was a bit strange, but when I shook his hand I felt good and everything appeared perfectly natural. My father didn't say anything, but I understood that I was supposed to go with him, and so we started walking along the avenue.

After a few minutes (to tell the truth, I don't know if it was a few minutes or much longer: time doesn't work the same way in dreams as it does when you're awake) we came across a big Alsatian lying asleep on the grass at the side of the avenue. When we came level, he got up and walked towards me, wagging his big, hairy tail. He let me stroke him and licked my hand.

It was a weird experience, because I'm scared of dogs, and if I see one in the street – especially if it's an Alsatian or another big dog like that – I certainly don't stop and stroke it. I was really pleased that I wasn't frightened.

"What's his name?" I asked my father, and that was when I realized he wasn't there any more.

My name's Scott, chief.

The answer appeared in my brain, and it was halfway between a voice that existed only in my head and a caption, like a speech bubble in a comic.

"You can talk?"

It's not quite true to say I can talk, chief. Actually, you can't hear me. This is my real voice.

And after he said that, he barked, which was a very deep sound, almost a growl, although there was something reassuring about it. And that sound I heard very well. In fact it was the only sound, apart from my voice, that I heard in the whole dream.

"Why did my father leave?"

Scott didn't answer the question.

Shall we go for a walk, chief?

He started moving and I followed him, even though I was a bit upset that Dad wasn't there any more. I thought, though, that if I'd met him once, it might happen again, and then we'd be able to talk.

Although it was a dream, everything seemed very real: I could feel the cool wind on my skin, I could smell the grass, and the sunlight, if I tried to look in that direction, was really blinding.

Then I remembered something I'd forgotten a long time ago. My father once said he'd buy me a dog. I just had to be big enough to look after it. I liked the idea a lot and asked him when, exactly, I'd be big enough, and he replied that eleven or twelve was the right age, because that's when you stop being a child and start to become a man.

As I was remembering this, I woke up.

I stayed in bed, waiting for my mother to come in and tell me it was time to get up and go to school. It occurred to me that it would have been great to have Scott with me during the day, to take him everywhere and maybe even have him come and pick me up from school. I'm sure some of the other guys would be much more careful about what they said and did if they saw me with Scott.

2

He turned the corner just in time to see her come out, walk a few yards, open the door of a car – a little runabout – and get in. Roberto walked slowly towards the front door of the building and was about to ring the bell when he heard a dull noise coming from the car, like the angry scraping of a jammed mechanism. He stopped his finger in mid-air just as it was about to press the button, turned, and walked towards the car.

The woman kept turning the key, and the same hostile, unpleasant noise kept repeating itself. Roberto knocked on the glass. The woman turned, looked up, fiddled with the window and finally opened it.

"It's the battery," Roberto said.

"Excuse me?" she said, her voice breaking slightly, as if she were trying to control herself and not succeeding.

"Your car battery's gone. That's why you can't start it, and can't even lower the window."

"So what do I do? Do I have to replace it? I'm in a bit of a hurry, I have an appointment. Maybe it's best if I call a taxi?"

"Don't worry. We can try and get it going. Or else we can find some cables and use the battery from another car."

He told her what to do. Sit down, switch the engine on, engage the clutch and put the car in second gear, keep the clutch engaged, let him push until the car has gained a little speed, and at that point gently release the clutch and press down slowly on the accelerator.

"I'll never manage all that," she said.

"You will. It isn't as difficult as it sounds. First of all press down the clutch pedal and turn the wheel as far as you can. I'll push you out of the parking spot."

She looked at him for a few seconds, slightly bewildered, but did as he had told her. When the car had moved away from the pavement, he went to the window again and repeated his instructions: "Keep the clutch engaged, switch the engine on, and put the car in second gear."

"But you can't push me all by yourself."

"Don't worry, it's a small car. When I tell you, release the clutch and put your foot down on the accelerator."

Then, without waiting for a reply, he started to push, and the car began laboriously to move.

"Release the clutch and accelerate," he cried from behind when the car had gathered speed.

The engine shuddered and the car jerked forward, coming to life with a raucous roar, went about a hundred feet and then stopped, but with the engine still on. Roberto caught up with it, and the woman looked out of the window.

"You see?" he said, slightly out of breath. "You did it after all."

"Thank you, you've been very kind." Then, as if she had forgotten an important detail, she stuck out her right hand and held it out to him. As they shook hands, he realized where he knew her from.

"Are you an actress?"

"Yes… I mean…"

"You did that commercial… the one for condoms… You were the pharmacist. You made me laugh a lot. You were… funny." He broke off, surprised at what he was saying. "I'm sorry, maybe I said something stupid."

"Don't apologize. I liked being funny, I liked making people laugh. It's been ages since anyone reminded me of that."

They looked at each other for a few moments longer, unable to find anything else to say, while the engine coughed.

"Well, goodbye then," Roberto said finally.

"Goodbye, and thanks again."

"Take the car to a garage."

"I will."

Roberto watched the car move away until it turned the corner and disappeared. Then he hurried to the doctor's office.

* * *

"Sorry I'm a bit late."

"You're out of breath."

Roberto gave a half-smile. "I just ran up the stairs, but before that I helped a woman to start her car. The battery was gone, so I had to push."

The doctor did not ask for any further explanation. "How was your weekend?"

"Not too bad. Actually, better than usual. I even went to the cinema."

"That's good. If my memory serves me well, you've never mentioned going to the cinema since our sessions started."

"You're right. I hadn't been. In fact, I don't even remember the last time I went. It must be ages."

"What did you see?"

"A French film, set in a prison. *A Prophet*. Do you know it? Have you seen it?"

"No, but I don't go to the cinema much either. Did you like the film?"

"I don't know. Some parts were realistic, showing the way things work in a prison. Others were completely absurd, though maybe I'm too influenced by the work I used to do.

But it was nice to go to the cinema. I mean, I'd forgotten what it was like, and I liked it a lot."

"Did you go to the cinema with somebody, or by yourself?"

"No, no. By myself."

"I'm very interested in the dream you mentioned last time."

"The one about surfing?"

"Yes, do you want to tell me about it?"

"The dream or the surfing?"

"Whichever you like."

"You remember I told you I was born and brought up in California?"

"Of course I remember. Your mother was Italian and married an American. Your father was a policeman."

"Yes, my father was a detective. We lived near the ocean, in a little town called San Juan Capistrano, between Los Angeles and San Diego."

"I imagine surfing's quite a normal activity for someone born and brought up in a place like that."

Was it a normal activity? Roberto couldn't remember – or didn't *know* – if it was so normal. For a long time, on the occasions when he went into the sea, he was the youngest in the group. A child, between the adults and the waves.

"I don't know, really. I was very attracted by the waves, from the time I was very small. I started at the age of eight, with my father. I went surfing with him and his friends. There weren't any other children."

"I remember seeing a film once, where a surfer goes right inside the tunnel created by the wave as it closes. Could you do something like that?"

"It's called a tube. Yes, I could do that."

They both fell silent. Now that the conversation had taken this unexpected turn, Roberto was trying to put his ideas in order and the doctor had that friendly but slightly enigmatic expression he sometimes had. An expectant expression. The silence lasted a couple of minutes, then Roberto resumed speaking.

"I really liked surfing. Even though I can't remember how it felt."

"What do you mean?"

"It's hard to explain, but I can't remember what I felt. I *know* I liked it – I liked it a lot – but I can't remember. I know, but I can't remember."

The doctor nodded. Roberto would have liked to know what he was thinking. He would have liked the doctor to provide him with explanations – sometimes he had even tried to ask him – but, especially in cases like this, the doctor didn't explain anything at all. Or rather, he didn't even speak. He just nodded. Or else looked him in the eyes. Or slid forward on his chair. But he didn't speak.

"When was the last time you went surfing?"

He couldn't remember. He tried to figure out when it had been, that last time he had surfed, but he couldn't, and that made him panic. As if there were a danger that everything might fall apart. As if the border between memories, dreams, reality, imagination and nightmares had suddenly broken down, and the yardstick for distinguishing one from the other had become intangible and pointless.

"I don't know."

"Is something wrong, Roberto?"

Roberto moved his hand over his forehead as if wiping away the sweat.

"I had the feeling I was losing control."

"You mean when I asked you when you'd last gone surfing?"

"Not when you asked me. When I realized I couldn't remember."

"Would you rather we changed the subject?"

Roberto hesitated. "No, no. It's fine now."

"Good. Even though you can't remember the last time

you went surfing, can we say it happened when you were still living in California?"

"Of course. I haven't surfed since we left California."

"How many years ago is that?"

"Oh, more than thirty years. I was sixteen when my mother and I left."

The doctor took a long Tuscan cigar from a drawer. From the same drawer he also took a penknife, cut the cigar in two, placed one half on the desk, and started playing with the other. This all lasted two or three minutes.

"All right. That'll be enough for today."

Roberto would have liked to add something. But the end of the session was always a moment he found hard to grasp. So after a few bewildered moments, he stood up and left.

Giacomo

I didn't dream for several nights, although that's probably not strictly true: I read in a science magazine that there's never a night when we sleep and don't dream. Apparently we dream every night, except that for various reasons, sometimes we remember and sometimes we don't.

So maybe it's more correct to say I don't remember what I dreamed for several nights, even though at least one night I couldn't have had very pleasant dreams, because I woke up with a feeling of sadness it took me a while to get over.

Last night, though, I went back to the park. Even when I was just about to fall asleep, I realized something was going to happen, and soon afterwards I found myself back on the same avenue as the other time, in the middle of the park.

Scott was sitting on the lawn, waiting for me. He was wagging his tail energetically as I approached, sweeping the grass with it. As I stroked him, I realized he smelled of shampoo and that he had a collar. I hadn't noticed it the first time, or maybe he hadn't been wearing it then. Anyway, the fact that Scott had a collar made me happy. It gave me the feeling he was really mine, not just a friendly dog I'd met by chance.

You're here at last, chief. I've been waiting for you.

"What do we do now, Scott?"

Let's go for a walk.

And without waiting for my reply he set off.

On this second visit, I managed to concentrate more on what was around me.

As I've already said, the avenue ran between lawns of high grass, across which the wind made big, silent waves as it passed. In some places on the lawn there were little hills, with quite steep slopes, like embankments on the sides of roads or railway lines. In the distance I could see a forest, which looked a bit scary, but only because it was far away. Every now and again we passed other boys and girls, many of them on foot, but some on bicycles.

After a while I saw a lake, with water so clear it looked like a swimming pool.

"Can people swim in that lake, Scott?"

That's what it's there for, chief.

I was about to ask him if we could swim straight away when I noticed a girl coming towards us. I recognized her, and the sight took my breath away. It was Ginevra.

Ginevra is a classmate of mine. She's the prettiest girl in the class; she has blue eyes, blonde hair and lovely dimples in her cheeks when she laughs. She's already had boyfriends, all much older than us, who come and pick her up from school on their mopeds.

I'm almost always distracted in class. I read books or comics – holding them under the desk – I draw, I write stories and thoughts in my diary, and quite often I look at Ginevra.

"Hi, Giacomo, you finally got here," she said, hugging me and giving me a kiss.

If Ginevra ever says anything to me in real life, I turn red and stammer and seem even more awkward and embarrassed than usual. So you can imagine how I'd be if she hugged me or actually gave me a kiss. In the dream I pulled it off a bit better than that, even though I was still excited.

"Is this your dog?"

"Yes, his name's Scott."

"He's lovely. It's one of the first times you've been around here, isn't it?"

"You… you mean here, in this park?"

"Yes, of course."

"It's the second time."

"I'm glad you're here. We never have time to talk at school. See you soon, OK?" She gave me another kiss – this one was closer to my lips and made me turn really red – and walked away.

"Scott, I have to ask you an important question."

Go on, chief.

"How can I make sure I come back here the next few nights?"

Scott stopped and looked at me, but I don't know if he answered my question, because just then I found myself in my bed with Mum shaking me and saying it was time to get up and get ready for school.

3

On Thursday, Roberto arrived almost half an hour early. He didn't realize until he was at the front door, and rather than wait outside – or, worse still, in the doctor's waiting room – he decided to go for a walk. Strolling slowly around the covered market in the Piazza Alessandria, a stone's throw from the doctor's office, he noticed an old drinking fountain with a thin but regular jet of water spurting from it.

In itself it was no great discovery, but at that moment it seemed like a revelation. Noticing that fountain, after passing it by for months, made him strangely cheerful. He washed his hands, stooped to drink a sip of water, and then resumed walking. The area was full of shops, workshops, bars and restaurants. He stopped outside a small pet shop and stood there looking at a few parrots, a fish tank and some Siamese kittens.

As he walked back to the doctor's office, he vowed to explore a bit more of the neighbourhood in the next few weeks. He sat in the waiting room for about ten minutes. Then the doctor said goodbye to someone, and the door leading to the exit opened and closed again. The exit was different from the entrance. When possible, that's how it works in psychiatrists' offices: you go in on one side and come out on the other; that way the patients don't meet. Waiting to see a psychiatrist isn't like waiting to see an orthopaedist, for example. No one has any problem admitting he has something wrong with his ankle or his knee. Nobody has any problem meeting an acquaintance in a dentist's or an ENT's waiting room. On the contrary, they have a chat and time passes more quickly.

But practically everyone has a problem admitting there's something wrong with his head. If there's something wrong with your head, you might be *mad*, and you have no desire to meet someone you know in your psychiatrist's waiting room, or when you leave after the visit – or rather, the session.

Hi, how are you? I'm a manic depressive with suicidal tendencies, what about you? I'm sorry, why are you looking at me like that? Oh, yes, I'm also your financial adviser and you're not all that happy to find out your financial affairs are being handled by a manic depressive with suicidal tendencies.

The doctor opened the door from his office to the waiting room, came out and stopped, surprised to see Roberto. "Here already?"

"Yes, I got here a few minutes early."

"It's the first time that's happened since you've been coming here."

The tone was neutral and it wasn't clear if the doctor was asking him a question or simply making an observation.

"I see you're in a good mood today. I'm pleased."

How does he know that? I was just sitting here, I only said a few words when I stood up, and I didn't even smile.

"Sit down. I'll be back in a few minutes."

The few minutes passed slowly. On the wall of the doctor's office, the wall Roberto always had his back to during the sessions, was a framed poster: a black-and-white photograph of Louis Armstrong laughing, with his trumpet in his hand, his arm hanging down by his side. The caption at the bottom said: *If you have to ask what jazz is, you'll never know.* Roberto wondered if the poster was new, or if it had always been there since he started coming.

"Is there a reason you got here early today?"

"No, I don't think so. Or rather, maybe there is a reason but I don't know what it is. I suppose there's a reason for everything."

"Not necessarily. Some things are pure chance."

He said this with a smile. Roberto thought it seemed almost a knowing smile, as if there were something else which there was no need to add because both of them already knew it.

"How are you today?"

"Fine." The sound of the word, as he uttered it, struck him as unusual, as if it had a new meaning.

"Well, better, anyway. For the last few nights I've been sleeping at least six hours, maybe even longer, and in the last two days I've smoked only five cigarettes in all. I'm still walking a lot and… Oh, I forgot to tell you before: I've started exercising again."

"That sounds like excellent news. What kind of exercise?"

"Nothing special. A few press-ups, a few weights."

Then, without knowing why, he asked the doctor if he practised any sports.

"Karate, ever since I was at university. I started because of this fellow who broke my nose in a stupid argument after my car bumped into his. I wanted to learn how to use my fists."

Roberto was surprised at this unexpected confidence.

"And did you learn?"

"To use my fists?"

"Yes."

"I don't know. I've never got into any fights with anyone. I imagine you can use yours."

He shrugged. Sometimes he'd used his fists, and sometimes, as a boy, he'd been at the receiving end of other people's. As a carabiniere, he had been involved in some fairly lively arrests, and sometimes in the station it had been necessary to calm down a suspect who was a bit too boisterous. Sometimes, too, it had been necessary to persuade someone to spill the beans without wasting a lot of time. He could clearly remember the face of a young man they had caught with some bags of heroin. He said he didn't know the name of the person who had given them to him and so he received a few slaps. Maybe a few too many. After a while he started sobbing. I didn't do anything wrong, he kept repeating. Roberto remembered the young man's face as he wept, and he felt a sudden, violent spasm of shame, as if for some unspeakably cowardly act.

"Before we continue, I wanted to tell you something."

"Yes?" Roberto said.

"You're getting better, we both know that. In a while we'll be able to start reducing the dosage of your medication. But don't do anything off your own bat. That wouldn't be a good idea."

"Actually I'd been thinking about that. Reducing the doses, I mean. Couldn't we —?"

"In a while. And you shouldn't worry about becoming addicted to the medication. There's no danger of that."

"Why?"

"Because you're afraid of becoming addicted, and that's the best kind of prevention there is."

He explained that the people who really ran the risk of becoming addicted to something – anything – were those who were convinced they could control the situation and stop whenever they wanted, whether it was drinking, smoking, taking drugs or gambling.

Roberto thought suddenly about cocaine, the fine texture of it, the white or pink colour, the slightly medicinal smell. He remembered it as if there were a heap of it right there in front of him, on the doctor's desk. The memory was like a slap.

He did his best to dismiss it. He nodded: he wouldn't change the doses.

"Now do you feel like telling me what happened after they took you on at the… what's the name of the department you were telling me about?"

"The criminal investigations unit."

"And what are its functions?"

"Much the same as the flying squad in the State Police. In other words, detective work. In a big city like Milan, it's divided into sections. Robbery, homicide, organized crime, corruption. And narcotics."

"And what section were you assigned to?"

"I did a few years in robbery and then they moved me to narcotics."

"Why was that?"

"There was more work and they needed more staff."

"There were more drug cases?"

"There are *always* more drug cases. Potentially, there's no end to them. The idea that you can defeat the phenomenon with carabinieri and judges and trials is complete nonsense. It's like thinking you can stop a wave by planting a stick in the sand. I'd never say this in public – none of us would ever say it – but the only way to wipe out the whole system and literally bring the Mafia to their knees would be to legalize drugs."

"But you didn't think that then?"

"You mean when I started to do that work? Of course not. I never thought we'd arrest them all and clean up society, but I was convinced I was part of the mechanism that would solve the problem."

"So what happened to change your mind?"

"We'd arrest ten people and confiscate, for example, two kilos of cocaine. After weeks or months of investigation. We had the feeling we'd struck a real blow, but from the point of view of the market it was as if nothing had happened.

29

Nothing *had* happened. The drugs continued to circulate, the dealers – not those ten, but others – continued to deal, and the customers continued to smoke and snort and shoot up."

He looked at the doctor to see what effect these words were having on him. He couldn't detect any – his expression was always inscrutable – but for the first time he noticed that the doctor had completely asymmetrical eyes: they were shaped differently, and one was noticeably bigger than the other.

"What exactly did your work consist of?"

"At first they stuck me in the intercept room, listening to phone calls about black and white T-shirts, trousers and jackets, and cream and chocolate pastries."

"I'm sorry?"

"Those are some of the terms dealers use to refer to drugs when they're talking to each other and they're afraid of being bugged. Or rather, let's say that they used to use. They've realized now that it's not such a good idea. I remember once two guys talking endlessly about deliveries of jackets, trousers and T-shirts. The deputy prosecutor asked us to check if the individuals really did deal in clothes, if they had warehouses or even just kept boxes of jackets, T-shirts and trousers at home. He wanted to rule out any possibility that they could defend themselves by saying they really were talking about clothes."

"And obviously there were no deliveries of clothes."

"Obviously not. Anyway, as I was saying, the first months were almost entirely intercepts and raids. Then I started working on the street, in discos and clubs."

"How do you mean?"

"Let me explain a few other things first. When we made arrests and took people to the barracks to do the paperwork before transferring them to prison, there were always a few colleagues who thought they'd take the law into their own hands and give the suspects a good going-over."

"You mean just beat them up without any reason?"

"Pretty much. Though they'd say that, since we were arresting them and then the judges were going to let them go, beating them up was the least we could do, from the point of view of justice, so that they didn't get the idea that it was all a joke and that crime was a risk-free business."

"Was it true about the judges?"

"Not at all. I never knew a properly conducted arrest – I mean an arrest without strong-arm tactics – that ended up in the criminals walking free. The truth is, most of the people doing the beating up just aren't very good detectives."

"But you told me you —"

"Oh, yes, I used my fists – sometimes you can't avoid it. It was the idea of beating someone up just for the hell of it that I couldn't take. When colleagues of mine worked a suspect over, I'd intervene and make them stop whenever I could. The suspect gets a good idea of who he's dealing with. They realized I was stopping my colleagues not because I was playing good-cop-bad-cop, but because I actually wanted them to stop. That was why a lot of them started to trust me. I'd see them when they got out, chat to them, I even became friends with a few of them. To cut a long story short, I started to build up a network of informants. Some of them I'd meet in discos and clubs where we could talk in peace. And in those places I'd get to know other people. They liked me and I made friends easily. Except these weren't normal friendships. I became friends with dealers, junkies, pimps, people like that. I'd been in narcotics for a year and I already had more informants than marshals who'd been working there for ten years or more."

Roberto realized that he was remembering a lot of these things at the very moment he talked about them. Or rather, only because of the fact that he had started talking about them. The time passed quickly, and for the first time the doctor did not notice until a bit later that the fifty minutes of the session were already up.

"All right, I think we'll call it a day. It's been very interesting. Keep taking your medication regularly, and I'll see you on Monday. I'm pleased with your progress."

Roberto stood up. As usual they shook hands at the door, with Roberto already out on the landing. He had started down the stairs when he heard the doctor's voice calling him.

"Oh, Roberto…"

"Yes?" he said, leaning on the banister and looking up.

"You look better with your hair and beard short. You did the right thing getting a haircut. Have a good evening."

The door closed before Roberto could think of an answer.

Giacomo

The morning after my encounter with Ginevra, I greeted her when I entered the classroom and tried to smile, which isn't something I usually find easy to do. She was surprised for a moment, but then she returned the greeting and even the smile, and I felt my legs go weak.

During the lessons, which I followed even less than usual, I wondered if by any chance she'd met me in a dream too. Maybe we'd both had the same dream, or maybe that park really exists and it's a place where people meet at night and become friends and things actually happen.

On second thoughts, I realized it was an absurd idea but at that moment, daydreaming in class, and especially after Ginevra had greeted me and smiled, everything seemed natural, everything seemed possible.

* * *

After a few nights of vague, meaningless dreams, I went back to the park. It happened a different way this time. I was under the blankets, after reading *The Neverending Story* for ten minutes. I'd switched the light off and closed my eyes for a few seconds when I saw Scott come in through the door and sit down at the foot of my bed.

I have to confess this apparition scared me a bit, partly because Scott wasn't saying anything. He just sat there, looking at me, and I even wondered if it was really him or another dog that looked like him. I felt almost paralysed: I'd have liked to get up or say something but couldn't. I don't know how long it lasted, but after a while Scott went to the window.

Let's go, chief.

What happened immediately afterwards I can't remember, but I assume I followed Scott, maybe by passing through the window.

What I do remember is that I found myself in the park again, walking with him by my side. Obviously in the dream I remembered what had happened and how we'd left my room, because I didn't ask him any questions about that.

"Scott, you remember the girl we met last time?"

Of course, chief. Very pretty, I'd say.

I was pleased that Scott had noticed, that in some way he was giving me his approval.

"Yes, she's the prettiest girl in my class. What can I do to meet her again? I mean, around here?"

Don't worry, chief. We met her once, we'll meet her again.

At that moment I smelled sweets in the air. Just like another aroma, from many years ago. Maybe I was three, four at the most. We were all together, Mum, Dad and me. I have very few memories of all three of us together. We were in a street somewhere, I'm not sure where. The aroma came from a street vendor, who had a handcart or a van, I can't remember which. What I do remember is that soon afterwards I was holding a hot waffle with cream and caramel, the best thing I've ever eaten in my life.

Before having these dreams I'd never realized that I miss my father.

4

The door opened and there she was.

"Did you take your car to a garage?" he said, making an effort to smile. He was out of practice.

"Oh, it's you. Yes, of course, I took it straight away and had to change the battery. I'm not sure whether I thanked you last Monday for your kindness. I can be quite distracted. Did I say thank you?"

"Yes, of course you said thank you."

"Well, at least that's something. I'm an expert at looking stupid."

"I think I was the one who made myself look stupid the other day."

"Why?"

"The way I blurted out that I remembered that commercial about… you know. Maybe you didn't like being recognized for that and —"

"No, no, I used to like doing commercials."

She spoke quickly, but without swallowing her words. As if some underlying nervousness wouldn't allow her to go at a calmer rhythm, but years of practice stopped her mangling the words.

"Why do you say 'used to'? Don't you do them any more?"

She shrugged, as if the subject was of little importance.

"I have to run," she said, after a glance at her watch. Roberto held back the impulse to tell her that he could walk her to her car in case it didn't start again.

"Then maybe we'll see each other again here."

She looked at him, uncertain how to classify that remark. "Maybe," she said at last, giving a slight smile and another shrug of the shoulders.

Then she started walking in the direction of her car and Roberto climbed the stairs. Only when he was outside the door of the office did he realize he had taken the stairs two steps at a time.

That hadn't happened in quite a while.

5

Roberto looked around. Louis Armstrong was still in his place, and on the other wall was a painting of a small fishing port, with boats drying in the low sun and a few figures. It was a painting that communicated a sense of peace: it's silent, Roberto told himself.

"Everything all right?"

"Yes, yes, I'm sorry."

"You were looking around."

"Yes, and I was thinking that for months I didn't even notice what there was in this room. Before, whenever I entered a place, I'd immediately register everything: the wider picture and the details. It was like I was photographing everything in my mind: once I'd been in a place I was able to describe it, down to the smallest detail. Whereas if in the past few weeks someone had asked me to describe your office, all I'd have been able to say was that there was a desk, two or three chairs, a small couch and a few bookshelves on the walls."

"And now?"

"Now I'm starting to notice what's around me. Outside and even inside. For example up until last time I hadn't noticed that poster. Unless you only just put it up. But it was there before, wasn't it?"

The doctor looked at the image of Louis Armstrong and smiled.

"Yes, it was. It's been there for a couple of years. Do you like it?"

"Yes… the words are… I don't know about jazz, I don't know all that much about it, but I think it's true in lots of cases: there are things you'll never understand if you need to have them explained."

For a few seconds, silence fell. Roberto was aware of a clock ticking loudly. He searched for it with his eyes but couldn't locate it.

"Shall we resume wherever we finished last time?" the doctor asked.

Roberto nodded, as if he had been called to order. He wondered if the doctor really didn't remember at what point they had broken off the previous Thursday or – more likely – if he was just trying to test his level of concentration.

"Yes. From now on most of my work took place at night, in discos and clubs. Apart from my first informants – and only very few of them – nobody knew I was a carabiniere. For the people who hung around those places, I was one of the many characters who spent their nights in clubs either killing time, picking up girls, or conducting various kinds of shady business."

"Forgive me if this question is a stupid one. But did you consider the time you spent in those places work time?"

"At first there wasn't a clear distinction. Then my superiors realized that my going to those places and rubbing shoulders with those kinds of people was generating leads for them. I was picking up items of news, telephone numbers, car registration numbers, addresses. I was talking to lots of people, and all the information I collected was leading to investigations, with surveillance, stake-outs, intercepts and all the rest. When the news was about the arrival of a consignment or the presence of narcotics in a particular place, we'd go straight in: raids, arrests, confiscations. Gradually my superiors started giving me more and more freedom, until I stopped keeping to strict office hours."

"Did you limit yourself to collecting the information or did you also take part in the arrests and everything else?"

"At the beginning, yes, when it was possible. Sometimes someone would tell me there were drugs in such-and-such an apartment, or at the back of such-and-such a shop. The place didn't belong to the person who had spoken to me, and when you do that kind of work, taking part in the raid and the arrests is important. It's a major part of the... How can I put this?"

"The job satisfaction?"

"Yes, that's it. The satisfaction. We've already talked about how arrests made me feel. But the deeper I got inside certain circles, the less advisable it was for me to be seen with my colleagues. In other words, as time passed, my work became more and more about being with dealers, pimps and traffickers, and less and less about listening to phone calls or conducting searches, confiscations and arrests."

"Did you immediately feel at ease in that situation?"

"That's a good question. Yes, I was at ease, and I think I liked it, but it's something I find hard to remember."

"Was it *enjoyable?*"

"Enjoyable?"

Enjoyable.

Had he enjoyed that period? Yes, probably, even though he would never have admitted it. But, whether or not it was correct to talk about *enjoyment*, he had liked that irregular life, where he was allowed to break almost all the rules of his normal work and the normal life of a normal carabiniere.

The doctor broke into his thoughts.

"Does the word bother you?"

"Maybe a little, yes. I'm not sure why, but it does bother me."

"Never mind. Carry on."

And maybe you could tell me why it bothers me. I mean,

I think it does, but you could explain why, you could try not always leaving things hanging, that way I'd have a clearer idea of what's happening inside me. He tapped his temple, as if to underline the meaning of a sentence he hadn't uttered out loud.

"As I was saying, I was inside that world now, and I'd built up quite a reputation as a criminal."

"Why?"

"Whenever the subject came up of what we all did for a living, I'd say I was in the import-export business. Without saying what exactly I imported and exported. Sometimes, though, I'd go into a bit more detail. Without ever being explicit, I'd mention South America, Colombia, Venezuela. The luxurious life I led when I was abroad, the important friends I had, things like that. Plus, I often turned up at these places in expensive cars that my colleagues and I were lent by car dealer friends of ours. And that naturally impressed people. Then there were the languages. Did I tell you that apart from English I also speak Spanish?"

"No. How did you come to learn it?"

"It's normal in California, especially close to the border with Mexico. And Spanish was the language of my father's family. His parents – my grandparents – were Mexican. They were the ones who emigrated to the United States."

"Oh, yes, of course. Your surname is Hispanic."

"One evening, one night rather, I was in one of these clubs, sitting at the counter with a girl, a prostitute who hooked her clients by asking them to buy her a drink. She was one of the people I'd got friendly with and we were having a drink – it was a slow evening for her – when this guy arrived who looked like he'd come straight out of a gangster film."

"In what way?"

"Dark suit, dark shirt, dark tie, thick sideburns, a gold cigarette lighter that weighed half a kilo, a gold watch that weighed a kilo. He looked like a caricature. He had these two gorillas with him who were obviously his bodyguards. They were caricatures too. Anyway, he said he wanted to talk to me. Alone. The girl – Agnese her name was, I remember it well – knew the score, and even before he'd got the words out, she'd already vanished. So this guy and I sat down at a table in a booth – the two gorillas kept their distance – and he ordered a bottle of champagne that cost three hundred thousand lire, just to impress me. A real clown."

"What did he want from you?"

"He asked me how come I spoke Spanish so well. Someone had heard me talking to a Venezuelan girl who worked in the club and had mentioned it to him. I made a vague reference to South America and the business I did there, which required a knowledge of Spanish. He gave me a crafty look, as if I'd said exactly what he was expecting to hear. He was congratulating himself on his own intuition. 'And what kind of business do you do in South America?' he asked, but as if he already knew the answer. 'Business where the first rule is to know how to mind your own business,' I replied, smiling and looking him straight in the eyes."

* * *

"Keep your hair on," the guy had said. He hadn't intended any disrespect, he only wanted to see if there was any possibility of their working together. It came out that the guy earned his living running a stable of girls, lending money, and occasionally handling small consignments of cocaine, intended for the same clientele as his girls. Now he'd been presented with an opportunity to take a qualitative leap. Someone had suggested he get involved with bringing in a major shipment of Colombian cocaine. He had immediately accepted and then immediately realized that this thing was much bigger than him, and the people involved much more dangerous

41

than those he usually dealt with, and he had started to get really scared. Beating up some poor bastard who didn't pay interest on his loan when it was due fell within his area of expertise. Handling his girls, gently when it was possible, violently when it was necessary, also fell within his area of expertise. They were things he knew how to do well, because he was a professional.

But when it came to the big time – and the thing he was getting himself involved in really was big time, as Roberto realized very quickly – he didn't know the score. Even though he didn't want to let the opportunity escape.

He had looked around, he had racked his brains, and in the end had remembered that determined-looking young man who was out and about almost every night, who seemed to know everyone, and who gave the impression he knew how to get by in certain situations.

"What exactly do you want from me?" Roberto had asked him to gain time. He was trying to get the situation into focus, feeling all the while like someone who goes fishing for sea bass and hooks a twenty-kilo tuna – and decides to reel it in. He really wants to reel it in, but he's afraid of breaking the line, so he proceeds cautiously. Very cautiously.

"If I've understood correctly – and I'm almost never wrong about people – you could assist me in this operation. It'll mean speaking Spanish, it'll mean —"

"Assist you?" Roberto interrupted him with a mocking smile and a hint of contempt in his eyes. "You mean I'd be your assistant?" He was enjoying playing this role.

The other man hastened to correct his blunder.

"No, I'm sorry, I didn't mean... I meant we could work together, as partners."

"How do I know you're not a cop and all this isn't just a ploy to frame me?"

"A cop? Me? Ask people about me, here or anywhere in

Milan, and you'll see if I'm a cop. Ask about Mario Jaguar and hear what they say."

"Mario Jaguar? Is that your nickname?" Another mocking smile.

The man's forehead and upper lip were covered with sweat, maybe out of indignation. There are people who really get upset when other people call them cops.

"Well, Signor Mario Jaguar, if you're so reliable you won't mind coming to the toilets with me and letting me search you, will you? After that, we can maybe talk business."

"What the fuck are you talking about?" There was a shrill note in his voice now.

"Well, you don't carry a certificate saying: 'I'm not a cop.' So before continuing this conversation I want to make sure that if I talk to you, I'm really talking *only* to you."

"What do you mean?"

"If you are a cop, you're a good actor. If you're not a cop maybe it's best you don't get involved in things that are bigger than you. Haven't you ever heard about microphones, wires, things like that?"

"You're mad."

"OK. Goodbye, then. It's best if you don't go into business with a madman."

So saying, Roberto got up from the table and made to leave.

"Hold on. Fuck it, you're touchy. All right, let's go to the fucking toilet and I'll let you search me. Maybe then we can talk seriously."

Roberto felt like laughing. It was an almost irresistible impulse, and he had to bite himself so hard to stop it that he made the inside of his lower lip bleed. As he entered the toilet, he had what amounted to a premonition. What was happening would change his life for ever. It only lasted a moment, but for many years Roberto would think of that moment as the real turning point in his story.

43

Obviously, Mario Jaguar wasn't wearing any microphones or wires. What he did have was an absurdly bulging wallet, full of large-denomination banknotes. They went back to the table and Jaguar ordered another bottle. The DJ had put on *Heal the World* by Michael Jackson, and a few unlikely couples were dancing in each other's arms.

"You know your job, don't you?" Jaguar said. "You searched me like a professional."

"Have you ever been searched before?"

"No, but —"

"Then how do you know how a professional searches?"

Jaguar's glass stopped in mid-air.

"Fuck it, you're no pushover, are you?"

Roberto looked at him without saying anything. Jaguar sustained his gaze for about ten seconds, then emptied his glass and filled it again. He lit a cigarette, took a drag, sniffed, and put the packet down on the table. Roberto took the packet and lit one for himself. He didn't really want it, but at that moment it seemed the appropriate thing to do for the part he was playing.

"Sorry I didn't offer you one. You didn't look like a smoker. Anyway, now can I tell you why I've been looking for you?"

"All right, go on."

He explained the reason. There were these Colombians he had been working with for some time, who brought him a dozen new girls every month. They were intended for regular customers who liked a change and had money to spend. He'd place the girls in a number of apartments in the city and work them round the clock for a few weeks. Then he'd send them off to other cities, either in Italy or elsewhere in Europe.

One day, one of the Colombians had suggested he come in on a cocaine deal.

"A major deal."

"What do you call a major deal?" Roberto asked.

"There's been this incredible increase in production in Colombia, and they're looking for new customers. They could send shipments of fifty kilos at a time, for a really good price, just because they have so much and they want to sell it off."

Roberto took a deep breath. Anyone looking at him might have thought he was weighing up the commercial possibilities of the information. In reality, the breath was a way to control his emotions. Shipments of fifty kilos? Nobody had ever seen quantities like that.

"It's the kind of thing that can change your life, a deal like that. I have my guys, I deal a bit of cocaine, but that's just half a kilo every two or three weeks. I give it to the same customers as the whores, plus some to friends. I don't know what to do in a situation like this."

"What did you tell the Colombian?"

"I told him I was interested but I had to talk to the partner I deal drugs with."

"But you don't have a partner you deal drugs with."

Jaguar smiled, assuming an expression of almost farcical cunning. He was clearly very pleased with himself.

"So you thought you'd talk to me and I could be your assistant."

"Hey, I already apologized, I used the wrong word. We'd be partners. The deal's fantastic. I have this contact and I have money to invest. You could manage things, go over there, meet these people, organize the shipment. Let's get together and split everything down the middle."

"You really don't want to miss this opportunity, do you?"

Jaguar laughed.

"Of course I don't. With quantities like that, we do a dozen shipments and then I can buy myself an island in the South Seas and I won't have to work for the rest of my life. And you can do the same."

Over the years Roberto would think about the bizarre, cruel situation Mario Jaguar had got himself in. Completely alone, doing everything on his own initiative. He had found the noose that would strangle him, and had stuck his head right through it, cheerfully drinking second-rate champagne at three hundred thousand lire a bottle.

"Do you have any ID?"

"ID?"

"A driving licence, an identity card, Mickey Mouse Club membership, whatever."

"Why?"

"Because before doing business with someone, I like to know who he is. Give me your ID, I'll make a note of your details, have them checked out by a few friends I have in the right places, and then we meet again here – let's say in three days – and talk some more. If you're straight, you have nothing to fear. If you aren't, just don't come back in three days. Of course, you could refuse to give me your ID, and in that case we've had a drink and a chat and we're friends like before. In a manner of speaking."

Jaguar sighed. Then he rose heavily from his chair, took his bulging wallet from his left-hand back pocket and extracted a crumpled driving licence.

"Will this do?"

Roberto took it without saying anything. He opened it and saw the photograph of a young man who wasn't yet called Jaguar, didn't yet traffic in whores and moneylending, and actually looked quite normal. The kind of person who's going to university or looking for a job, who goes out with his girl for a pizza or to the cinema, who plays football with his friends, who gets a photo done for his driving licence in an automatic booth. And then his life suddenly takes a turn, and he's transformed into Mario Jaguar, pimp, moneylender and aspiring (but unlucky) international drug trafficker.

Roberto called the waitress and asked for a pen. Actually he had one with him – he *always* had one with him – but he didn't want to arouse even the slightest suspicion. Why should an international trafficker, a professional criminal, be carrying a pen? A pen is what a cop uses to write down what he sees so that he doesn't forget it, but a criminal doesn't usually need a pen. If he does need one, he borrows it.

After noting down on a paper napkin the particulars of Mario Binetti, known as Jaguar, Roberto gave him back the licence.

"I'm going now. If everything's OK, we'll meet in three days, same time, same place. If things aren't OK, it's best for both of us if we don't meet, either here or anywhere else."

"We'll meet and we'll do business and thanks to me you'll become rich. If you have any contacts in the police they'll tell you who Mario Jaguar is. I give some of them a free turn with some of my girls every now and again and in return they let me work in peace."

Roberto had to restrain himself from asking who these officers were. One thing at a time, he told himself, mentally mouthing the words. First the drugs, then, if possible, his corrupt colleagues.

He stood up and left. As he walked through the door of the club, he was thinking that what had happened to him was incredible, and that he should make an effort not to run, not while he could still be seen. Running wildly to work off your excitement isn't the kind of behaviour expected of a high-class criminal, an international trafficker. Which was what he was about to become and would remain for more than ten years.

* * *

The doctor looked at his watch.

"I confess even I'm having to make an effort to finish on time today."

47

Roberto didn't know where he was going with these stories. But he had the impression he had found a direction.

He left the building and, as he headed home, he noticed an old-style restaurant and pizzeria where he was sure he must have been more than once, some years earlier. Good pizza, really good thick fries.

It had definitely always been there, even in the past seven months.

6

Sometimes remembering and thinking are not beneficial activities.

The doctor had often told him that. We mustn't allow ourselves to be trapped by our thoughts or memories. When they come, we have to look at them objectively and let them fade away.

Thoughts stay with us only if we hold on to them, he would say. By way of explanation, he had cited the example of a trap used in a particular region of India to catch certain types of monkeys. The way the trap works is simple but deadly. It's a kind of pot with a narrow opening and food inside. The opening is just wide enough to allow the monkey to put his hand in, but stops him taking it out with his fist closed. So when the monkey grabs the food and then tries to get his hand out, he can't. If he let go of the food, he'd be able to free himself, but as he won't let go, he's trapped.

A nice story, Roberto thought. Evocative and perfect.

In theory.

In practice, how do you let go of your thoughts when they're planted in your head like nails, and the more you try and get them out the more they tear your soul?

But then, with time and thanks to the progress of his therapy, and also the medication, the suggestion had started to seem less impractical. For example, whenever he walked, concentrating on taking one step after another, he had the feeling those sticky lumps of suffering became less stubborn and for a few moments actually melted away, and his head became delightfully free. What the doctor had said would happen actually happened, and his thoughts, those solid entities made up of memories, recriminations and decaying dreams, slipped away, even if only for a short while – long enough, though, for him to realize that it was possible.

When he got home, it occurred to him that in two months he would have to have a medical check-up. It was the first time he had thought about possibly going back to work.

The first time since a colleague had found him in the office, at night, with a gun in his mouth, wondering if you really didn't feel any pain when you shot yourself in the head at such close range. Wondering if they would find him with shit in his trousers, like the murder victims he had seen, or if the instinctive, split-second fear of dying would kick in before the nine-millimetre Parabellum bullet went right through his brain and smashed his skull.

He was very calm, very clear-headed, as he felt the taste of the burnished steel on his tongue and wondered what the scene of his suicide would look like.

He distinctly remembered the expression on the face of that young officer, the terrified expression of someone who would like to run out to find help but realizes that this might well be the wrong move. Definitely the wrong move.

"Please take that thing out and move it away." He actually said *please*, which Roberto thought was interesting. Please don't shoot yourself in the head. Apart from getting the office dirty, it would all be a complete mess: lawyers, journalists, inquiries.

Please take that thing out of your mouth. Please, I became a carabiniere because I wanted things to be straightforward, with the bad guys on one side and the good guys – us – on the other. Clear, straightforward, predictable.

There was no provision for finding a colleague in the office at two o'clock in the morning, ready to blow his brains out.

Roberto looked at him with genuine curiosity, feeling an unreal sense of calm and control. The young officer had a smooth, boyish face: he couldn't have been more than twenty-five and looked as if he was about to burst into tears.

"Please take it out and put it on the table." His voice was shaking.

Roberto wondered what to do. Press the trigger or put down the gun? For a few moments he felt a sense of complete omnipotence, of infinite possibilities. He was the master of life and death. He could choose.

Choose.

He took the barrel out of his mouth and put the gun on the table. It was cocked, and it would only have taken a very slight pressure to produce an irreversible result.

"Can I come closer?" the young officer asked.

"Of course," Roberto replied, somewhat surprised. Why on earth shouldn't he come closer? he thought, once again in a complete, coherent sentence.

"Can I take it?" the young man asked when he was level with the table.

"Wait," replied Roberto. He picked up the gun and gently pressed the hammer, rendering it harmless. He detached the magazine, pulled back the slide and tipped out the bullet that had been waiting in the barrel, ready to go through his brain.

"Now you can take it," he said at last. "You have to be careful with these things. It doesn't take much to go off and cause a tragedy." His voice was neutral, with no hint of irony or sarcasm. It didn't sound like – it wasn't – the voice of someone who, just a minute earlier, had been hovering between life and death.

The young carabiniere took the gun, the magazine and the bullet that had been expelled when the slide had been pulled back. Then at last he went out and called for help. Roberto sat there waiting.

* * *

The mind had to be kept occupied, that was the thing. That way it was easier to avoid becoming prey to your thoughts.

Cooking is almost always a good solution. Roberto made himself an omelette, concentrating hard on every step of the recipe.

Letting the omelette cool down, he opened a bottle of wine.

A little wine, in moderation, was compatible with his medication. All the leaflets said that the effect of medicines could be exacerbated by being combined with alcohol, but the doctor said a glass of wine a day was allowed, although spirits could certainly wait until the therapy was complete.

After dinner, he switched on the TV. Another rule was not to go channel-hopping. He needed to learn how to concentrate, even if it was just on watching a film or television programme from beginning to end. If there was nothing worth watching, it was better to switch off and do something else. Actually, that was easier said than done when you had satellite TV. If there weren't films, if there weren't any interesting programmes, at least there was always sport, especially basketball, the NBA. That evening the Los Angeles Lakers were playing the Minnesota Timberwolves. A boy growing up in southern California, providing he doesn't hate basketball, is bound to root for the Lakers, at least a little. Basketball is perfect for killing time, for filling the space between dinner and the hour when the body starts to accept the idea of going to bed.

More than two hours passed in this way. The familiar, over-excited voices of the presenters, the lightning-fast passes, the gold jerseys and black muscles, the slam dunks, Jack Nicholson in his courtside seat as usual, the commercials for Taco Bell, Subway, Chrysler. The Kiss Cam conferring a few seconds of worldwide celebrity on couples kissing in the crowd.

The Lakers won by twenty points. The Timberwolves weren't exactly the most formidable opponents in the NBA, but the result still put him in what was almost a good mood.

Time for bed. Time to brush his teeth, rinse his mouth and wash his face, while avoiding looking in the mirror and seeing his lines and his extra pounds.

Maybe five minutes on the computer, just to glance at the daily papers.

His attention was drawn to news of an international anti-Mafia operation. Members of the Calabrian Mafia, the 'Ndrangheta, had been arrested in Australia, and the fact that Mafiosi from Calabria had become firmly established on the other side of the world was presented as a new and disturbing development.

But wasn't it common knowledge that the 'Ndrangheta was now in Australia, just as it was in many other places throughout the world?

Maybe for those in his line of work; obviously not for journalists and everyone else. And anyway, he corrected himself, that was his *former* line of work.

It was at that moment that he realized he was talking to himself out loud, asking himself questions and answering them. He wondered when he had started, but couldn't find an answer to that one – "I really couldn't say, my friend" – and concluded by telling himself it probably wasn't anything serious, although he might tell the doctor about it the next time.

When he had finished browsing the news, he did not switch off the computer. He went back to the home page and typed in the name of those condoms and the words *commercial* and *pharmacist*. The video came up immediately. She was visibly younger, her face was beautiful and funny, and the commercial still made him laugh.

From there, it wasn't difficult to click through to other sites and other videos. Roberto discovered that her name was Emma – he repeated the name a couple of times and decided that it suited her – and that she had done films and TV as well as a lot of commercials.

He was wondering why none of the videos were recent when he came across a commercial for mineral water. He had never seen it before. She was bathing in a pool of sparkling water, full of little bubbles. She was in a bathing suit and was pregnant, with a large taut belly on her girlish body.

One of the things Roberto found impossible to do was look at the naked belly of a pregnant woman. Or rather, he found it impossible to look at a pregnant woman, whether naked or clothed.

So he switched off the computer, took his sleeping pills, and went to bed.

7

That Thursday, Roberto arrived early again and went for another exploratory walk around the neighbourhood. He discovered that the Museum of Contemporary Art was located a stone's throw from the doctor's office, in an old building that had once been a brewery.

How many times had he walked right past it? It was a bit bigger than a drinking fountain, and yet he still hadn't noticed it.

He told himself he must go in one of these days. Then he walked on a bit further and discovered a little shop that sold second-hand records and sheet music. The hand-painted sign read *Lizard King*. Behind the counter, sitting at a computer, was a man with grey, shoulder-length hair, a leather jacket and a flowered shirt with an oversize collar that rested on his lapels. He looked about sixty and gave the impression that his stylistic development had stopped at the beginning of the Seventies. He looked up just long enough to see who had come in and then looked back at the screen.

Roberto browsed through the old CDs and vinyl with a slight sense of euphoria, as if he were looking for something specific and was about to find it.

When he had finished his inspection, he told himself he couldn't leave without buying something. He picked *Nevermind* by Nirvana. As he went out, it struck him that the neighbourhood was becoming familiar, which was a comforting thought.

* * *

"I see you've been shopping at *Lizard King*."

"Oh, yes, I looked in and found this CD. It's music I remember hearing at the time of the story I'm telling you, that's why I thought of getting it. Strange guy, the owner."

"Yes, he is a bit weird. Apart from selling second-hand records, he writes reviews in specialist magazines. He's not exactly outgoing, but he's friendly enough when you get to know him."

"Even the name of the shop is strange. *Lizard King*. What does it mean?"

"It was Jim Morrison's nickname."

"The singer from the Doors?"

"Yes. Do you like the Doors?"

"I don't know much about music. Is 'Light My Fire' by them?"

"Yes. Maybe you know this one too." He gave a pitch-perfect whistle that seemed to be produced by an electronic instrument.

"I know the tune but I can't remember the title."

"'People Are Strange.'"

"You whistle very well."

The doctor shrugged and gave a little smile.

"What kind of music do you like, Roberto?"

"I don't really know much about it. I used to listen to whatever was around, but now that you've asked me the question, I don't think I could say what kind of music I like. And I haven't listened to any for a long time. I can't even explain why I bought this CD. I know I told you I bought it because it was music I heard at the time of the story I'm telling you, but if we hadn't talked about it I'd probably have taken it home, put it down somewhere and forgotten all about it."

"But now you'll listen to it?"

"Yes, I will."

The doctor nodded his approval, as if with that reply an important subject had been dealt with in the best possible way and now they could go on to something else.

"The story about the man who wanted you to help him ship cocaine from Colombia," he said. "How did it end?"

"We met in the same club three days later, as we'd agreed. I'd informed my superiors, and in agreement with the Prosecutor's Department they'd decided to mount an undercover operation. It was still fairly rare in those days. We dug up everything from our files that we could find about Signor Mario Binetti, known as Jaguar, and by the time I saw him again, I knew more about him than he knew about himself."

Roberto broke off, following an idea that had crossed his mind.

"I'd done my research and enjoyed discovering every detail on the person I was going to be dealing with. Studying people and situations was maybe the thing that interested me most. Arriving perfectly prepared, knowing everything about the people I was talking to."

"I imagine the work of a good detective revolves very much around identifying people's weak points."

"That's right. Everyone has a weak point; you just have to discover what it is. I remember this guy from Apulia who was on the run. We knew he was in Milan, and we'd been looking for him for quite a while. We were under pressure, the Prosecutor's Department wanted us to find him because they were convinced that once they had him he'd turn State's evidence. Which, incidentally, turned out to be correct. We were sure he was in the area but we couldn't locate him. Nothing from the phone intercepts, nothing from tailing his family. But talking to one of my informants, it came out that this guy was obsessed with raw mussels."

"How do you mean?"

"I mean he really liked them. Someone from his home village near Bari owned a fishmonger's in Milan, and our man had been in the habit of going there to eat mussels before he went on the run. My informant told me about it by chance, but when I heard that, a light went on in my head. So, without saying anything to anybody, apart from the colleagues on my team, I organized a stake-out of the fishmonger's. Two days later we picked him up."

"I should pay you for telling me these stories," the doctor said with a smile.

Roberto shrugged, as if to downplay it. But he liked the doctor's admiration. It was something new, and he liked it a lot.

* * *

He and Jaguar became friends. Or rather, Jaguar persuaded himself that they had become friends. They met the Colombians, and discussed prices and shipments. Roberto said he could guarantee safe passage in a couple of ports, thanks to his export company and his friendship with some customs officials who were happy to supplement their income. The export company was created for the purpose, and the roles of the corrupt customs officials were taken by two other carabinieri who had been assigned to the operation and provided with covering documents.

During one of their briefings, someone observed that Roberto couldn't be accepted in criminal circles without having even a single tattoo. There are a few professional criminals who don't have tattoos, but they are an exception to the rule. The absence of tattoos was the kind of thing that might attract someone's attention. Roberto didn't much like the idea of getting a tattoo, but he managed to convince himself, and when the moment came to choose what to have carved on him he opted for the head of a Red Indian chief on his left forearm and a spider's web on his right shoulder blade.

"Are you sure you want the spider's web?" asked the owner of the tattoo and piercing parlour where a colleague had taken him: the man was a former fence who'd done time. "You do know what it means, don't you?"

"No, what does it mean?"

"The spider is a predator. In some circles, having a spider or a spider's web on your shoulder – on your elbow it's different – means that you're someone... who's spilled blood and is ready to do it again."

Roberto thought it over and then said that the spider's web would be fine. The tattooist shrugged.

"All right. I have to do you another one anyway."

"Why?"

"Tattoos must always be odd numbers, otherwise they bring bad luck. If you like I can do you a nice ACAB on the knuckles."

ACAB is an acronym for All Cops Are Bastards.

He didn't know if the other man had meant to be witty – he knew that Roberto was a carabiniere – or if he was being serious.

Roberto laughed, although he felt he was becoming unpleasantly enmeshed in something that was already getting out of his control.

"All right, do me an ACAB. But not on the knuckles – find another place that's less visible. And I don't want any colours; do everything in black and white."

It was more painful than he'd anticipated. By the time they left the laboratory – that was what it was called on the little sign outside – a few hours later, Roberto had a strong burning sensation in his shoulder, forearm and calf, which was where the acronym about cops being bastards had ended up. Now he was ready to enter his second life, which would soon become his first life.

The Colombians liked him: he was down-to-earth, professional, friendly, and spoke excellent Spanish with a vaguely Mexican accent.

Jaguar invested all his savings in the operation, dreaming about the tropical island he'd buy with the proceeds of this new activity.

But there were to be no tropical islands or even any proceeds for Jaguar, or for his men, or for the Colombian envoys who had come to Italy to follow the final phase of the operation and collect the agreed payment. After six months of negotiations, inspections and journeys back and forth, they were all arrested, and a ship, its hold stuffed with several billion lire worth of cocaine, was confiscated in the port of Gioia Tauro.

Roberto's first operation as an undercover agent. The beginning, as they say, of a brilliant career. A few months later they offered him the chance to join ROS at their headquarters in Rome.

ROS is the Carabinieri's special operations group, dealing mainly with organized crime and terrorism. The aristocracy of detectives, the highest a young officer who likes investigative work can aspire to. Roberto naturally accepted, was transferred, and soon afterwards was sent to the United States to follow an FBI course for undercover agents.

After he came back, he would rarely wear his uniform again, and then only to receive commendations.

* * *

"I'd noticed the tattoo on your forearm, but I would never have imagined the reason you had it done."

"It was a bit difficult to imagine."

"Haven't you ever thought of having them removed?"

"At first, yes. I thought that as soon as I finished working undercover – I took it for granted it would only be temporary – I'd have them removed. Then time passed, I kept doing undercover work, and I actually grew fond of the tattoos. Even the ACAB, which after all is true in a way."

The doctor made no comment and looked at his watch.

"Have we finished?" Roberto asked.

"We still have a few minutes."

"I have the impression that everything is moving around me."

"And before?"

"Before, everything seemed still."

"I'd say that's good news."

Roberto would have liked to ask why it was good news. But he didn't do so. Instead, his gaze wandered around the room and came to rest on the poster of Louis Armstrong.

He realized why it was best not to ask: if you need to have something important explained to you, you will probably never understand it.

Giacomo

For a week, I was in bed with flu. I don't mind being ill, because then I don't go to school and I can read as much as I like, without worrying about homework.

Reading is probably the thing I like the most, and if I'm really forced to answer the question about what I'd like to be when I grow up, I'd say I want to be a writer. Or rather, to tell the truth, I'd like to be a writer even before I grow up. My model is Christopher Paolini, who started writing his first novel – *Eragon*, which I've read twice – at the age of fifteen.

Anyway, I was saying I'd been at home ill. I don't remember what I dreamed during that week, but I definitely didn't go to the park and that worried me a bit.

When I got back to school, however, a surprise was waiting for me: Ginevra had noticed my absence. When we met in class, before the first lesson, she said, "Oh, you're back at last." I searched for a witty reply, but couldn't think of anything better than: "I had flu, but I'm completely over it."

That made me a bit nervous, but I was very pleased, because she'd noticed my absence and had spoken to me before I could speak to her. Immediately after that, though, Cantoni welcomed me back in his own way, with a slap on my neck from behind.

Cantoni's a moron. He's five foot seven and a brown belt in judo. I'd like to react to his bullying, but I'm barely five feet tall, and the only thing I could beat him at is ping-pong, which I'm quite good at.

* * *

That night I went back to the park. I found myself there in different circumstances from the other times. I was having a nap lying on the grass, in the shade of a tree, when Scott came and woke me up.

I know it seems really strange to talk about having a nap during a dream, but that's how it was, and there's not much you can add.

Let's go, chief, they're waiting for us.

He set off quite quickly and I was forced to run after him to catch up.

"Wait for me, Scott, slow down. Where are we going?"

He didn't reply, just kept trotting along.

"Who exactly is waiting for us?"

Still no reply. I was starting to get irritated and I walked faster to catch up with him, stop him and force him to answer me – was I or wasn't I the chief? – when I saw a bench in the middle of the lawn and Ginevra sitting on it. Scott stopped about fifty feet away and lay down on the grass.

Go on, chief, she's waiting for you.

I approached the bench and Ginevra gestured to me to sit down next to her.

"That Cantoni's a real idiot," she said.

"I don't mind," I said, as if to imply that, if I wanted, I could react and destroy Cantoni and the only reason I didn't was because I don't believe in violence.

"You know I have a boyfriend, don't you?"

I nodded.

"Do you have a girlfriend?"

"Oh, I've had a few," I lied in a nonchalant tone. "But right now I prefer being alone."

"Yes, I don't think I'm going to stay with my boyfriend much longer either. There's someone else I like a lot more." As she said this, she looked me straight in the eyes. I swallowed with difficulty, and couldn't find a single word to say in reply.

"Do you have someone you like?" she went on.

"Well, yes, there is someone I like a bit…"

"Is she pretty?"

It struck me that I should immediately stop playing the fool and tell her the truth, that I was in love with her and we mustn't waste another minute.

When Mum woke me up, she said I'd been repeating that sentence in my sleep: We mustn't waste another minute.

She asked me what it meant. Why mustn't we waste another minute? I sat up, yawned, and said I'd been dreaming but I'd already forgotten the dream.

8

On Saturday evening his colleague and friend Carella had invited him to dinner.

Carella was plump and almost bald. He had three children, his wife was the same girl he had been going out with when he was seventeen, and he spent his free time doing charity work for a parish association in the Pigneto district, where he lived. He was in the criminal investigations unit, and despite appearances – which as is well known are deceptive – he was an excellent detective.

He and Roberto had met at the officers' training academy, and although they were very different they had remained friends over the years.

Carella had taken Roberto's situation to heart: he phoned him at least once a week and invited him to dinner once a month. It was impossible for Roberto to get out of these invitations without offending his friend and so, more or less once a month, on a Saturday evening, he submitted to the ritual of dinner in the Carella household. Carella's wife was there, as well as two of his three children (the oldest, being nineteen, went out and avoided the obligation), the apartment smelled of Marseille soap, they ate badly – Signora Carella specialized in overcooked pasta, whatever the sauce – and they talked about old times. Roberto would converse politely without hearing what they were saying to him, or even what he himself was saying, waiting for the moment when it wouldn't seem too impolite to take his leave.

This evening had been like all the others. When they were at the door, saying goodbye, Carella told him, as he always did, that he was looking better. This time, though, he added something else.

"You know, Roberto, over these months I've always told you you were looking better, that you were making progress and that everything would soon be back the way it was. Do you remember?"

"Of course."

"Well, it wasn't true. I said it to help you, to cheer you up, but I didn't think you looked well at all. Not even a bit. You were always distracted. So distracted, I sometimes felt like asking you what I'd just said, and I was sure you wouldn't have been able to tell me."

Roberto looked at him with genuine curiosity.

"Tonight was different."

"In what way?"

"You were here. Not always, of course. But at least there were times when you were here and your eyes were the same as they used to be. In the past few months you seemed... well, you were different, but tonight I'm really pleased. I can tell you you're looking better without telling a lie."

Roberto did not know what to reply, nor did he really understand what his friend was referring to. The evening hadn't seemed any different from the others. He gave a slight smile – which could mean anything – and Carella returned it. When things aren't clear, it's easier to get by without words.

He walked back on foot, as usual: walking quickly, it took about an hour to get from the Pigneto to his apartment.

As he was crossing the Piazza Vittorio he saw a young guy trying to open the door of a car that clearly wasn't his. Fifty or sixty feet from Roberto, another young guy stood lookout.

Without a second thought, Roberto walked to the car and the youngster playing with the lock.

"What are you doing?" he asked, immediately thinking he'd seldom asked a more stupid question in his life.

The young man looked at him in surprise. Clearly the question had struck him as strange, too. "I'm stealing," he said at last, in the tone of someone who thinks everything is far too obvious to require further explanation. Roberto felt like laughing and had to make an effort to control himself.

In the meantime the lookout had also approached.

"I'm off duty and on my way home," Roberto said. "Don't force me to do my job. Just drop it and go."

The two young men stared at each other for a moment, looked Roberto in the face, obviously decided it wasn't worth taking the risk, and disappeared into the night.

The next day was sunny, and Roberto took a long walk as far as the Foro Italico. He ate in a trattoria somewhere and then returned home, still on foot. He told himself that he should measure the distances he covered – and then immediately wondered why on earth he would do that.

He remembered those words of Louis Armstrong. *If you have to ask what jazz is, you'll never know.*

Every now and again he glanced at the phone to see if by chance anyone had called him without his having noticed. It was an absurd thing to do, because people hardly ever tried to get in touch with him these days, and it certainly hadn't happened this Sunday. And yet he had the feeling the impulse meant something. Figuring out what was quite another matter.

He spent half the afternoon and evening watching TV and the other half on the computer.

He looked again at some of the videos he had seen a few days earlier, although he avoided the commercial for mineral water. He found some new ones, including extracts from stage plays, in which Emma looked very different.

All of a sudden, he had the nasty feeling that he was using his computer as some kind of giant keyhole, through which he could spy without being seen. It seemed to him that he was violating a space he could only legitimately enter with the permission of the person involved.

The thought made him feel uncomfortable, and so he abruptly cut off the connection, switched off the computer, took his medication and went to bed.

9

The next morning Roberto woke up very early, before dawn. He tried in vain to get back to sleep, but he was feeling too restless, so he got up, dressed, ate a few biscuits, drank a glass of milk and went out, moving quickly as if he were late for an appointment.

He walked along the Via Panisperna, turned into the Via Milano, quickly reached the Via Nazionale, and by the time he circled the fountain in the Piazza Esedra he was almost running. He got to the Porta Pia, went through it, and it was not until he was in the Via Alessandria that he realized he was very close to the doctor's office. Except that there were another eight hours to go before his appointment. It was only then that he eased the crazy rhythm of his walk, continued for another half an hour, and found himself inside the Villa Ada park.

The first thing he noticed was that there was a drinking fountain near the entrance, similar to the one he had seen a few days earlier. The discovery gave him a quiver of joy.

He should have been feeling tired, he thought, instead of which he felt a kind of excess of energy, something that needed releasing and working off. He descended a slight, grassy slope and looked around to see if there was anybody about. Obviously there were a few people, even though the park was half deserted. Who cares, he told himself, everybody comes here to exercise, and he started doing press-ups.

He did them until he collapsed face down. When he got up again, his arms were shaking and he found it hard to control his breathing.

An elderly man with an Alsatian on a lead was looking at him anxiously. There were other people exercising in the park, but in tracksuits and trainers. Someone doing press-ups in jeans and a regular jacket was unusual to say the least. When the owner of the Alsatian realized he had been spotted, he looked away. Obeying an instinctive impulse, Roberto walked towards him.

"Good morning," he said in a cordial tone when he was almost level, trying to recover his breath.

"Good morning," the man replied, somewhat puzzled. The dog was following the scene, its senses alert.

"Alsatians are my favourite dogs," Roberto said.

The old man seemed to relax. "Mine too. I've always had Alsatians, ever since I was a little boy. They're the best."

"Yours must be three or four years old."

"You have a good eye. He's actually three and a half."

"Isn't he a bit of a handful when you take him for a walk?"

"You mean that because I'm old he might drag me or make me fall?"

"No, I didn't mean that, I —"

"Don't worry, it's a perfectly reasonable question. I'm eighty-one. If he decided to send me flying he could do it easily."

"But he doesn't."

"No, he doesn't. He's a good boy, very well trained."

"Trained by you?"

"Yes. Training dogs was my hobby when I was younger. I was quite good at it, I took part in competitions and often won."

"What kind of competitions?"

"Do you know something about them?"

"A bit. I'm a carabiniere, I've had quite a bit to do with dogs."

"Ah, I used to have quite a few friends in the Carabinieri's canine unit. I've lost touch with all of them; I have no idea if they are still alive. Anyway, I took part in competitions in the utility and protection categories. The last one I went in for must have been about twenty years ago."

It was a neutral phrase but he seemed suddenly overcome with emotion. It was as if he were looking into the distance but couldn't find what he was searching for.

"Does he let people stroke him?" Roberto asked at last.

"If I give permission," the old man said, with a hint of pride. And then, turning to the dog: "It's all right, Chuck, he's a friend."

The dog started wagging its tail soberly and approached Roberto, who stroked its head and then scratched it behind the ears.

"Can I ask you a question?" the man said.

"Of course."

"Why were you doing press-ups in your street clothes like that?"

"I looked a bit strange, didn't I?"

"Actually, you did."

Roberto shrugged.

"I'm just coming out of a very difficult period of my life. There was an earthquake and now I'm dealing with the aftershocks."

The old man looked at him with an expression of aroused curiosity and nodded as if he had understood, but maybe – Roberto thought – he was only trying to be kind.

"Well, I have to go. Congratulations on the dog, he's very beautiful."

"If I were your age I'd try not to waste time. We never get back a single minute that we waste. Good luck."

Roberto said goodbye and the man left, the dog walking perfectly in step with him, like a soldier happy to follow orders. Roberto had the impulse to go after the man, stop him and ask him to explain what he could do so as not to waste a single minute. Of course he didn't. He stood there watching the man walk away, thinking that, like most of the people he had met in his life, he would never see him again.

* * *

He arrived at a quarter to five. He went into the bar opposite the doctor's office and ordered a juice, keeping his eye on the building. He had just come out and was crossing the road when the front door opened.

"It seems we have a date," she said smiling at him.

Roberto responded to the smile, while thinking, with a vague sense of panic, that he did not know what to say.

"It seems we do."

"It occurs to me we haven't even introduced ourselves. My name's Emma."

Roberto held out his hand, and told her his name.

"I already know your name. Maybe I shouldn't have, but I had a look at some of your videos. From what I gather, you're very good."

He spoke quickly, as if fearing he wouldn't be able to say everything he wanted. She did not seem either touched by the compliment or annoyed by the intrusion.

"At my best, I *was* good. I mean, I wasn't bad, but that's my old life. I don't act any more."

Roberto managed to hold back the question. What was she doing now? Better not to ask questions when you don't know what they might lead to. A lawyer friend had told him that once. It was a rule of trial procedure, but it was obviously valid in many other cases.

"I saw that you also acted in the theatre."

She seemed thrown, as if the subject made her feel uncomfortable, or at least was completely unexpected.

"Do they have those things there as well? I mean, can you actually find those videos on the Internet? I never use it, just sometimes for e-mail."

"I saw that you acted in Shakespeare," Roberto insisted, but as soon as he had finished the sentence he felt awkward and stupid. He had spoken in the confident tone of someone who goes to the theatre and knows all about Shakespeare.

The only times he'd ever set foot in a theatre in his whole life was when he'd been to a few concerts – apart from once, to arrest a couple of prop men who supplemented their income by dealing cocaine in theatrical circles. That was the one occasion he'd actually seen a play. If his memory served him correctly, it was by Pirandello and, while he was there in the darkness, something in the dialogue had struck him.

"Do you like the theatre?"

Here it came.

"To tell the truth, I haven't seen much. But yes, the little I have seen I liked. I like Pirandello." There, he'd said it. Now she would ask him what he liked by Pirandello, he wouldn't be able to reply, he would look really stupid, and she would realize what a slob he was.

"I was once in *As You Desire Me*," she said. "We toured Italy with it." From the faraway look in her eyes it was obvious it was something she had long forgotten that had suddenly come back into her mind.

Roberto nodded his head slightly, with the expression of someone who is perfectly familiar with what is being talked about. He hoped intensely that she would change the subject, and swore that this evening he would go on Wikipedia and find out all about Shakespeare, Pirandello and that play, the title of which he had memorized: *As You Desire Me*.

"The kind of things that come up when you meet someone by chance," she said at last. Mentally, Roberto sighed in relief.

73

"Now I really must dash. Actually, I always have to dash. Next time you could tell me what kind of work you do. Bye."

She passed in front of him, wrapping her scarf around her neck and leaving behind her a slight smell of perfume. Roberto watched until she had disappeared around the corner and then went inside the building.

10

Climbing the stairs, he told himself there could be no doubt: Emma, too, was one of the doctor's patients. When a coincidence is repeated, it constitutes first a clue, and then evidence. It was a prosecutor Roberto had often worked with who had loved repeating that sentence, but now that he came to think about it, it wasn't as profound or original as all that. Not at all, in fact.

For some obscure reason, this thought put him in a bad mood.

"Is there something wrong today, Roberto?"

Obviously, the doctor had noticed. Roberto had the childish impulse to contradict him.

"No, no. It's only that last night I had a dream that made an impression on me and I was just thinking about it."

"Tell me about it."

That was it. He had no dream to tell.

"I dreamed that I met a woman. She was someone I'd seen before, and the encounter happened in a familiar place, but I can't quite pin down where it was. We talked, she told me her name, and then she rushed off. And as she rushed off I could smell her perfume, which is strange for a dream, isn't it?"

He was surprised at himself for how he had concocted the story. It was all true and all false, he told himself. Like lots of other things, come to think of it.

"Actually, smells in dreams are an unusual experience. But it does happen. What name did this woman give you in the dream?"

"I don't remember. I don't remember what she said, but it was as if we were introducing ourselves and then she had to run because she was in a hurry."

"And can you identify the smell? Did you like it?"

"I couldn't say exactly. It was a light perfume, and in the dream it struck me that she probably only put on a little. But I liked it, yes."

Why was he getting all tangled up in this nonsense? He had never before lied to the doctor, and now he was trying to interpret a non-existent dream. What does it mean to dream about a smell? Or a meeting with a woman who runs away? He felt guilty.

Immediately, though, and for a few long, disconcerting seconds, he wondered if that encounter a little while earlier had really taken place. The experience, brief as it was, made him feel dizzy.

"Has that ever happened to you before? I mean: to have dreams that involved smells?"

"If I have, I don't remember."

Now please let's change the subject, he thought.

"If dreaming about a perfume is a novelty for you, then I'd say we have a piece of good news. Another sign of development."

The human mind works in a surprising way. There was no dream and so this whole discussion ought to have been meaningless. And yet when the doctor told him that it was good news, that the smell meant things were changing for the better, Roberto believed it. The light perfume that Emma had left behind her was good news for him.

"I realized something this weekend. I've been dreaming a lot more over the past ten days. Really a lot. I never used to dream before. All right, I know, a statement like that doesn't mean anything. We all dream every night, you told me that."

"You did dream, but you couldn't remember. In a way, though, the phrase *I didn't dream* is correct."

Roberto looked at him, waiting for an explanation.

"Do you know the story of the tree that falls in the deserted forest, where there's nobody to hear it crash to the ground?"

"No."

"Imagine an old tree, with its trunk all rotten and eaten away by parasites, which gives way eventually and crashes to the ground, among the other trees, destroying branches, sweeping away bushes and maybe rolling once it's fallen. Imagine there's nobody in the forest to hear the tree fall and crash."

Roberto was looking at him, puzzled.

"Do you follow me?"

"I'm trying."

"If there's nobody to hear it fall, does the tree make a noise?"

"How do you mean?"

"If there's nobody in the forest or in the immediate vicinity, and so nobody hears the noise, can we say it existed?"

"The noise?"

"Yes."

"Obviously I'd like to say yes, but I assume it's a trick question."

"There's no trick. Did the noise exist or not?"

"Of course it existed."

"How do we know if nobody heard it and —"

"What has that got to do with —"

"Wait, let me finish. How do we know if nobody heard it and there's nobody to tell the story?"

Roberto did not reply immediately. This was no chance provocation on the part of the doctor, and so, in all probability, the most obvious reply wasn't the right one. In the past, the doctor had mentioned the fact that paradoxes help us to understand reality and solve problems. Especially those of a disturbed psyche.

"Do you mean that if no one hears it, the noise doesn't exist?"

"It's an old Zen riddle, which also has a scientific basis, though I'm not going to bore you with that. The function of Zen riddles – they're called *kōans* – is to confront the pupil – in this case, you – with the contradictory, paradoxical nature of reality. They help to draw attention to the multiplicity of possible answers to the problems of existence and aim to awaken consciousness. In some ways they have a similar function to the practice of analysis."

"So?"

"So thinking about the question of the tree in the deserted forest may prompt you to think about dreams and about what it means to remember them or not to remember them."

"But what does it mean?"

"The Zen master rarely responds to such a direct question. The idea is that the pupil, in searching for the right answer, finds himself. In other words, self-knowledge."

At that moment, there was an explosion of yelling from somewhere in the building. A man and a woman were arguing. Of the two, it was the woman who was shouting more loudly and angrily. The man seemed to be on the defensive, and was about to give in. Roberto wasn't sure if the voices came from the apartment above or the one below.

"They're downstairs," the doctor said, guessing Roberto's question.

"Why are they arguing?"

"Because they've reached the end of the line but can't summon up the courage to admit it."

In the meantime, the shouting had stopped. Roberto felt an incomprehensible sense of anguish about that private tragedy being played out downstairs. He thought about those disintegrating lives and those hearts filled with resentment and the things those two must have imagined for their future together.

"Do you know something?"

"What?"

"I'm sorry for those two. I don't understand why, but I really feel sorry for them. As if I knew them, as if they were friends of mine."

From the apartment downstairs came the noise of a door being slammed, but no more voices.

"Am I mad?"

The doctor made a gesture with his hand, as if to brush away something that was bothering him.

"We all have our share of madness. The question is how we live with it. Some manage quite well, others don't. People come to me to learn to live with their own madness. Even though almost nobody is aware of it."

The words should have scared him. Instead, Roberto felt an unexpected sense of calm. Like something that could be accepted and which, when you confronted it, was much less unpleasant than when you imagined it hidden in some fetid compartment of your consciousness.

"There's something I've never asked you, Roberto."

"Yes?"

"Do you like reading?"

It was strange that he should be asking that question now. A little earlier, Roberto had been thinking that he ought to find out something related to Emma's interests. Do some research on the Internet but also read something. To be ready to talk to her without feeling that he was on shifting sands.

"I can't say if I like reading. I haven't really read much. Whenever I have, sometimes I liked it, but reading has never been a habit of mine."

"Do you remember what you liked?"

What had he liked? He couldn't remember. He did recall a good book on the history of basketball that he had read a few years before, but that didn't seem the most appropriate thing to mention. He realized that he was trying to look good in front of the doctor, and that he was ashamed of his own ignorance. More or less the same feeling he had had less than an hour before, talking to Emma.

"A few years ago I read a book about lies that a lawyer had given me. It was by an American psychologist..."

"Paul Ekman?"

"Yes, that was him. They also did a TV series about him."

"*Lie to Me.* The book you read was probably *Telling Lies.*"

"Yes, that's the one. In a way, I even applied it to my work. I mean it gave me a few ideas."

"What about novels? Do you ever read novels?"

Novels. He couldn't remember if he'd ever read a novel in his life, which probably meant he hadn't. And anyway, when would he have had time to read novels? At the age of nineteen he had joined the Carabinieri. The course, then the first posting, the work, always more of it and always more intrusive. In his free time, of which there had been less and less, he had done other things. Most of them things he didn't like to remember.

"It's no big deal if you don't like novels."

"I don't think I've ever read one. It was never something I thought about. Now that I realize, I feel ashamed."

"Shame can be a useful feeling. It's a sign that something's wrong and it can be a stimulus to change for the better."

Roberto felt like crying. He was forty-seven years old, most of his life had passed and fallen to pieces, he had nothing left to show for it. He was a failure, a lonely, ignorant, unhappy man who had lived in a senseless way.

The doctor's voice interrupted this unbearable sense that everything was slipping away.

"Let's do something. Now the session's over, if you have nothing else to do, go to a bookshop – choose a big one, they're more suitable for those who need practice – and spend a little time there. Look at whatever books you like – sports books would be fine too – and when you find one that looks interesting, buy it, take it home, and read it. Then, if you feel like it, we can talk about it next time."

11

The doctor had suggested a big bookshop. He remembered there was a really big one in the Largo Argentina which he could easily reach on foot from the doctor's office in less than half an hour.

He walked quickly, as usual, and it took as much time as he had anticipated. Outside the entrance, two Africans tried to sell him some books of fairy stories and he had to make a bit of an effort to refuse, walk round them and go inside.

Once inside, he realized he didn't know how to behave. Whenever he had been into a bookshop in the past, he had always done so for a particular reason. A specific book, to buy for a specific purpose. Go to the assistant, ask for the book, take it to the cash desk, pay and leave. Without even *seeing* all those other books, thousands of them, on the shelves, on the tables, even on the floor.

He looked around cautiously, as if the others might notice him, realize he was a stranger here, and start whispering among themselves while watching him suspiciously. It took him a few minutes to convince himself that nobody was paying any attention to him. More generally, people seemed to be ignoring each other. They were walking around between the books and the shelves, browsing, selecting, going to the cash desk or else leaning against a bookcase, sitting down on a little sofa and reading for a long time as if this was a library.

The sight of these people reading without paying at last managed to relax him. If nobody was paying any attention to them – and nobody was, not even the assistants – then nobody would pay any attention to him.

He started focusing on the microcosm around him. Up until that moment he had been aware only of masses, some colourful, some dusty, and individuals moving between those masses.

There was a group of men in grey suits and loose ties; a boy photographing the cover and a few pages of a book with his mobile phone; an elderly lady examining the crime section with a professional demeanour; two girls talking non-stop, apparently completely uninterested in books or anything else apart from their conversation; a man with a beard like an officer in the Alpine troops, looking at history books and every now and again sniffing and loudly clearing his throat.

After wandering for a few minutes in the middle of all this humanity, as if in an aquarium, Roberto asked an assistant to point out the section for theatre books. Maybe, he thought, he'd find something there that would give him a few ideas for what to talk to Emma about. But none of the titles he looked through seemed suitable. There were plenty of play scripts, of course. Roberto pulled out a volume of Beckett, read a page, and emerged feeling anxious. Then there were volumes about the theatre with titles like *For a Shamanistic Theatre* or *The Empty Space*. He tried leafing through these too, and again gave up quickly.

Next to the theatre books was a section of books about writing, and among these Roberto was drawn to a manual entitled *How to Write the Story of Your Life*.

As he leafed through it, he noticed a fat man in a dark baggy raincoat looking at him furtively. He had a book in his hand and a rucksack on his back – which seemed tiny on that bulk – and as is often the case with fat people he was

83

of indeterminate age. After a few seconds, he put the book back on the shelf and approached Roberto.

"May I ask you a question? You might think it's indiscreet, and you can just tell me it's none of my business, I'll apologize, and that'll be the end of it."

"Go on."

"You don't spend much time in bookshops, do you?"

Roberto felt a twinge of annoyance, and for a moment thought of telling him that it genuinely wasn't any of his business. "Is it that obvious?"

"Actually, yes."

Then he held out his hand and introduced himself. He said he was a journalist, and was supposed to be writing a series of pieces on people who frequented bookshops. The regulars and the occasional ones. Roberto had immediately struck him as an interesting subject.

"Do you mind if I ask you why you came in here today?"

Explaining everything, Roberto thought, could be a little complicated.

"I met a woman who loves the theatre," he said. "I'd like to buy her a book, but I have no idea what to get."

It was a lie, but as he said it Roberto had the impression he had discovered the real reason he had ended up in here.

"Buy *The World's a Stage*," the man said, taking a book with an orange cover from a table and handing it to Roberto. "It's a very good book about Shakespeare and his period, entertaining and serious at the same time. It'll impress your lady friend, even if she's already read it. In fact, maybe even more so if she's already read it."

Just at that moment, a scruffy-looking woman approached, holding a volume with a dark blue cover, and asked the fat man if he could sign it for her. The man smiled, said yes, took out a cheap pen that looked small in his hand and wrote something on the first page. The lady thanked him, apologized for the interruption, and went back to a friend who was waiting for her about ten feet away.

"I sometimes write books too," the man said in a vaguely embarrassed, almost apologetic tone. They stood there without saying anything else. The arrival of that woman had disturbed the balance. In the end the journalist-writer broke the silence, said goodbye – nice to meet you – and headed, as rapidly as his bulk allowed, towards another part of the shop.

Roberto looked at the cover of the book he was holding in his hand and then headed for the cash desk.

He felt like a fish out of water, but pleasantly so. In fact, he felt quite light-headed.

12

The light-headedness did not last long and soon gave way to anguish and a sense of emptiness. An alternation of excitement and depression. He and the doctor had talked about that some time earlier. For a few weeks or a few months the two states might well alternate as the situation improved.

But was it really improving?

By the time he went to see the doctor, on Thursday afternoon, his thoughts were mostly grim ones.

"Did you go to a bookshop?"

"Yes, I went as soon as I left here."

"And was it a positive experience?"

Roberto hesitated for a few seconds. Positive. Yes, it had been, even though he was in a bad mood today. But those were two distinct things.

"Yes, I'd say it was. I met a journalist. Actually, I then discovered that he's also a writer."

"A writer? What's his name?"

Roberto told him about his trip to the bookshop and the encounter with the journalist-writer whose name he couldn't remember – from the description the doctor seemed to figure out who he was, but said nothing – and the only time he hesitated was before replying to the question about what he had bought.

"A biography of Shakespeare."

If the mention of Shakespeare had any effect on the doctor, he didn't let it show.

"So all in all, you liked your visit to the bookshop?"

"Yes, and I went back home in a good mood. It lasted one day and then yesterday I woke up early in the morning with an unpleasant feeling."

"What kind of feeling?"

"Sadness and fear. Almost as strong as the first few times I came here. And from yesterday morning until today, my mood has only got worse. I thought I was getting better, but now I'm scared. I feel as if I don't have any control over what's happening inside here." He gave himself quite a hard tap with his hand on his forehead.

The doctor took a deep breath, rolled up the sleeves of his dark cotton shirt over his slim, muscular forearms, and cleared his throat.

"We've already talked about that, and I'm sure you remember. These things never have a linear progression. You take three or four steps forward, then two back, then a few more forward, and so on. The backward steps derive from a fear of change. If we live with suffering for a long time, it ends up becoming somehow part of us. When we start to feel better, when we start to detach ourselves from the suffering, we experience contradictory states of mind. On the one hand we're pleased, on the other we feel uneasy, because we're missing something that was part of our identity and guaranteed us a kind of balance. That's the reason for this fluctuation between euphoria and sadness. It's normal, there's nothing to be scared of. No more than there is in the fact that you're alive and in this world, of course."

"Maybe that's the problem. I'm scared of living in this world."

"I think you need to be more trusting. When a situation gets better, in other words changes, we feel the jolts. It's normal for a few days of genuine euphoria to be followed by moments that are less euphoric. In our jargon, we call them dysphoric moments. When they arrive it's a bit like ending up under a wave. The basic rule is not to panic, not to resist, because it's pointless, and wait for it to pass."

"Does it pass?"

"Almost always. Anyway, you of all people should know what it's like, ending up under a big wave."

"You completely lose the sense of your position. You don't know what's up and what's down. You don't have any control over your movements or over your own body."

"As if the rules of space were suspended?"

"Yes, that's it exactly. As if the rules of space were suspended." Roberto repeated the words slowly.

"And how do you get out of it?"

"You have to wait for it to pass."

"Precisely. It's the same thing. Sometimes, if the wave is particularly big, if the fall has been violent, I assume some help can come in useful."

"Yes. But I always pulled through by myself. Even if it was hard sometimes."

"Do you think you'd have been able to do that with any wave?"

"No, you're right. There are cases where you can't pull through without a helping hand. And sometimes you drown anyway, even if there's somebody to help. It happened once to a boy I knew."

"Sometimes it happens, yes. Unfortunately and despite the efforts of whoever's trying to help."

"Anyway, it's just like you said. You have to surrender to the wave, when it comes, without getting in a panic. After a few seconds, almost always, the world returns to its place."

"Do you want to tell me a bit about surfing? You told me you started with your father."

"Yes."

"Any good?"

"Me or him?"

"Both of you."

Roberto felt as if he'd been caught off balance, as if all at once he'd lost his footing. The words did not come at first, and he moved his hands as if searching for some kind of support.

"My father... was good. Old school, but very good. He'd surfed with some of the best, people who'd ridden really big waves, in Hawaii, at Waimea Bay on the North Shore."

Roberto broke off abruptly.

"Obviously, these names won't mean anything to you."

The doctor made a gesture with his hand as if to say: it doesn't matter.

"What about you? Were you good?"

"I got by."

"Is that the most accurate description? *I got by*?"

Roberto looked at him.

"I was good. In fact I was very good, I might even have been better than my father if I hadn't stopped."

The doctor smiled. A real bittersweet smile, as if they were two friends chatting over a beer and one of them had remembered something nice that united them, one of the reasons they could say they were friends.

"I once read a novel that featured surfing, and I remember a sentence that struck me. It went something like: 'It's one thing to wait for the wave, and quite another to get up on the surfboard when it comes.'"

"Whoever wrote that sentence knew what he was talking about. When you're there you realize that all the rest is bullshit. I'm sorry, doctor, but bullshit's the only word for it. You have a feeling of truth, I don't know how to put this, the sense that everything is... brought into focus. A feeling of beauty, of totality, of being one with everything else. When the wave

89

carries you, you feel you're *part* of it, if you understand what I mean, you feel that everything finally has a meaning. And when you're on certain waves – which are like mountains of water, actual mountains – you don't care about anything. You just want to find out what you're made of. Nothing matters except being up there. And there's a perfect harmony, in those seconds when you're there, a balance between the sea and the sky, almost still, while you slide very fast between the water and the air, and the roar. You pass through the middle of the wave, exactly equidistant from those opposites."

Roberto broke off, stunned at how the memories had come out and had transformed themselves into a story.

"Do you believe in God, doctor?"

The doctor looked at him with a hint of surprise on his face. He took a while to answer.

"Do I believe in God? Have you ever heard of Blaise Pascal?"

"No."

"Pascal was a seventeenth-century French philosopher. A philosopher and a great mathematician. He's famous, among other things, for his so-called theory of the wager."

"What's that?"

"Pascal said it's worth wagering on the existence of God. I'll spare you his full argument, but basically the idea is that if we wager on the existence of God, and God exists, we win the wager and our gain is infinite. If God doesn't exist, we don't lose anything and at least our life has been made happier by faith. According to Pascal."

Roberto tried to get the hang of the idea. It was attractive, but also somehow elusive.

"There's something I don't quite get," he said at last.

The doctor did not reply. He was looking at him, moving his head slightly, with his lips shut. He seemed to be trying to maintain control of a situation that had developed in an unexpected way.

"Are you afraid of death?" Roberto asked.

"Strictly speaking, I ought to tell you that my opinions on the afterlife, or my fears in this life, aren't subjects we can talk about here. Strictly speaking."

"I'm sorry."

"Having said that, and forgetting about *strictly speaking*: death isn't my favourite thing to think about, I admit. But the really troublesome idea is all the things that may lead up to it. I'd like to spare myself those."

"I'm starting to remember a few things from when I was a child and a teenager."

"Tell me."

"I remember the chewing gum dispensers, those round coloured balls of chewing gum. Do you remember them?"

"Go on."

"Well, I remember the chewing gum and I remember peanut butter. And Snickers, and marshmallows… and I also remember a time when my father took me to see a Lakers game."

"The Lakers are a basketball team, right?"

"The Lakers are the best basketball team in the world. One of the Los Angeles teams. My team."

He seemed to smell the popcorn, and hear the roar of the crowd in the Forum when Kareem Abdul-Jabbar shot one of his famous sky hooks, and feel the paper Coke cup in his hand. He remembered his father's tartan jacket, his moustache. He seemed to see him, as he talked to him with his smell of aftershave and cigarettes.

They were commenting on a particular play in the game, or maybe talking about something else. Roberto was following the scene like an outside observer and did not hear what the two of them were saying. After a while the man gave the boy a comradely punch in the shoulder, and Roberto didn't think he'd be able to hold back. Very soon he'd start crying and he wouldn't be able to stop.

"My father was a detective, as I've told you. We lived in the suburbs. From our house to the sea was ten minutes maximum. A few minutes more to Dana Point, which is a great place for surfing. My mother was a translator. Early one morning, my father's colleagues came knocking at the door and took him away. It was a beautiful day, a Saturday. We were expecting some fantastic waves that morning. A few days later, he killed himself in prison. I remember hardly anything about the following weeks, but six months later we moved to Italy, to my mother's family's apartment. She'd inherited it a year or so earlier from her parents. She and my father had intended to sell it. My mother never went abroad again for the rest of her life. I never went back to California."

He said all these things in a flat, colourless voice. The doctor took a deep breath. Roberto felt a sudden anger rising inside him – aimed, unexpectedly, at the man in front of him.

There were a few minutes of heavy silence.

"Obviously you're not going to ask me why my father was arrested," Roberto said at last, still angry. "But if you don't ask me I won't tell you. I'm a bit fed up with playing a game where you're the only person who decides on the rules."

"Why was your father arrested?"

Roberto made an impatient gesture.

"He'd been taking money from the owners of bars, restaurants and nightclubs. If they paid him he left them alone; if they didn't, he made things difficult for them."

And then, after a pause: "I've never told this to anyone before."

"You would have stayed in California, wouldn't you?"

"Yes. You know something absurd?"

"What?"

"I'm angry with my father not so much because of the offences he committed, but because he killed himself and left me alone. Damn him."

He stopped speaking. He twisted his hands for a long time, scratched his chin, rubbed his face.

And then the tears arrived.

Giacomo

Now Ginevra and I say hello to each other every day, when we arrive at school and sometimes even when we leave, if she's not in too much of a hurry. Then yesterday, something new happened: she called me by my first name.

Her exact words were: "Giacomo, do you have a spare pen? Mine doesn't write."

We were in the middle of an Italian exercise, and put like that it may not seem like anything important. She only asked me for a pen, and what can you call someone except their name?

At school, though, we almost always call each other by our surnames, and we only use first names with those who are real friends. And that means it *is* important.

I thought I ought to reply by calling her by her first name, which I'd never done before. In our class only two friends call her by her name. I couldn't do it, but in the next few days I swear I will, one way or another.

I also thought I'd like to make a compilation for her of some of my favourite songs, which are all from before I was born. Things my parents used to listen to, like the Rolling Stones, Led Zeppelin, Dire Straits. I'll put them on a memory stick and find a way to give it to her. Of course, it won't be easy without anybody seeing me, but I'll deal with that when the time comes.

I have to admit it: I think I have a mad crush on Ginevra.

* * *

Last night Scott took me to the lake, the one with the transparent water that's like a swimming pool, and he told me we could bathe there. I dived in head first – now that I think of it, I was fully dressed – and glided like a fish for several yards under the surface of the clear blue water. I should say one thing immediately: I don't know how to dive in head first and, even though I can swim, more or less, deep water scares me, like so many other things.

In the lake in the park, it was different. I felt safe and I swam a lot, with my eyes open even though I was under the surface, and I could see just as well as if I had a mask on. Scott also dived in and swam with me, we played, and it was all great fun. When we came out of the water, we were dry, which, seen from this side, may seem strange, but at that moment felt perfectly normal.

"Scott?"

Yes, chief?

"This is a dream, isn't it?"

I think so, chief.

"I ask because sometimes it all seems so real."

Scott sat down in front of me and looked at me, tilting his head to the side, waiting for me to ask him whatever I wanted.

"If I do or say something on this side can it have an effect on the… real world?"

I had the impression that Scott smiled before answering.

Almost everything that happens in the real world depends on what you do and say on this side, chief. And vice versa. Not many people know that, but that's the way things are.

What he said was a bit mysterious and I'm not sure I quite understood what he meant. I tried to concentrate, but the more I tried to grasp the significance of those words – and what they might have to do with me, and with Ginevra – the more elusive they were.

Then everything became blurry and in the end I woke up.

13

He got back home after his long walk on Saturday evening, had a shower and made himself something to eat. As he was waiting for the pasta to cook he happened to glance at the package from the bookshop, which had been there in the kitchen for some days. Absently, he took out the book he had bought for Emma and read a few pages at random.

It didn't seem bad, the story of the mysterious William Shakespeare of Stratford-upon-Avon. Almost unaware of what he was doing, he started reading from the beginning and carried on until late at night. He resumed reading the following morning, continued in the afternoon and that evening in bed. He finished about midnight and found that the experience had been unusual but interesting. He had read a whole book in one day, and it had all seemed quite natural. It was the very naturalness that was the most extraordinary thing about it. He had always considered reading to be an activity that required commitment, planning, time. Something reserved only to those who could afford it. Now it turned out that reading was – or could be – like drinking, eating, walking or breathing.

There must be a meaning to all of this, he said to himself, switching off the light and pulling up the blanket, and a moment later he was asleep.

When he woke up on Monday morning and looked at the clock, he realized that he had slept soundly for nearly nine hours, without interruption.

The last time that had happened must have been twenty years ago.

* * *

It started raining as he was on his way to the doctor's office, and within a few minutes dark-skinned umbrella vendors had materialized on the street corners. Roberto bought an umbrella, thinking he would add it to the collection he had at home: one for every rain shower that had caught him out in the last few months, the end of winter and the beginning of spring.

He got to the office at twenty to five. He had anticipated walking up and down outside the front door until she came out. That seemed less natural with all this rain coming down. He thought of taking shelter in the bar opposite but immediately dismissed the idea. She would come out through the front door and, seeing the rain, would immediately run – towards her car or somewhere else – in order not to get wet. So the only way to get to talk to her a bit was to wait for her in the entrance hall. The idea embarrassed him a bit, but there were no alternatives. He rang the bell for the office, nobody replied, and as usual, after a few seconds the door opened.

He waited for about ten minutes without anybody going in or coming out. Then at ten to five he heard someone coming downstairs. It was quite a nimble, almost masculine tread. Roberto was wondering if it wasn't somebody else when Emma emerged from the last flight of stairs. She saw him before she got to the bottom and stopped on the stairs, with a surprised expression. Then she descended the last few steps more slowly.

"Hello," she said when she reached the foot of the stairs.

"Hello."

"It's raining really hard."

"Yes, it came down all of a sudden, but I bought an umbrella."

"If this was a screenplay, that last bit of dialogue would have to be rewritten. We can do better."

"You're right, but you intimidate me."

"I don't know if I should take that as a compliment."

"I think so. May I ask you a question?"

"Yes, of course."

"Are you a patient…?"

"Yes, and so are you, aren't you?"

"Yes. But I must tell you I'm quite harmless, and not mad. Not very much at least. Are you mad?"

It had come out well. She burst into sudden laughter. A nice full laugh.

"Sometimes I think I am. I thought I was in the past, but now I think it's getting better. No, I really don't think so. I'm not mad, though the doctor says we all are."

"Yes, I know, the difference is between those who can live with their madness and those who can't."

"Then you're doing well. You're almost cured."

"Why?"

"The doctor only told me that when I was starting to get better, many months after the sessions started. At the beginning, I don't think I would have understood."

"Do you think it's wrong of us to be so friendly?"

A new laugh, shorter but similar in tone.

"Why not? After all, we are colleagues."

"Colleagues?"

"Both psychiatric patients," she said with a laugh.

"I have a book for you."

"A book for me?"

Roberto took the volume from the pocket of his raincoat. What he told her was almost the truth. He had gone to a

98

bookshop – he didn't mention it was a new experience for him: that was an aspect of the matter that could best be left in the dark – and seen this book which had been recommended to him by a friend, had read it and liked it and had thought she would like it too. Only much more than he did. Provided she hadn't already read it.

Almost the truth.

She looked at him in surprise.

"I've heard of this book. I was planning to read it. Thank you."

She reached out her hand and took the book he was holding out. And then after a brief pause, as if she really couldn't hold back: "How strange."

"What is?"

"You didn't seem the type... I mean you didn't seem the kind of person who'd read something like this. I may be putting my foot in it, as usual, but what I mean is you seem more like a man of action than someone who reads this kind of book. If you were in a film, for example, you'd more likely be a policeman than a teacher."

He smiled without saying anything. She looked at him questioningly. He kept smiling without saying anything.

"You aren't actually a policeman, are you?"

"I'm a carabiniere."

"No."

"Yes."

"But you look... You're the first carabiniere I've ever met."

"I've never met an actress before either."

She gave a slight grimace. It lasted a very short time and she probably hadn't even been aware of it. She moved her head as if to rid herself of a troublesome thought.

"I'm not an actress any more. Now go, or you'll be late."

"Do you have an umbrella?"

"No."

"I'll walk you to your car."

"You'll be even later."

He did not reply, walked out, opened the umbrella, and nodded to her to follow him. The rain was beating down harder than before, so hard that there was almost nobody in the street. Emma leaned close to him to get under the shelter of the umbrella. The mere contact of her hand on his arm sent a quiver through him.

Identical – he thought, astonished that such a distant memory should well up so powerfully out of nowhere – to the quiver he had felt so many years earlier, on the dodgems, when a girl the same age as he was – fourteen – had placed her hand on his leg.

They reached the car. She opened the door while he protected her and got wet in the process.

"Well," she said, "thank you. Let's hope it isn't raining next Monday."

"Yes, let's hope so," he said, feeling like a fool.

"Bye then, officer."

"I've written my telephone number inside the book. Just in case."

"Oh, good."

"Bye then."

"Bye."

* * *

"I'm sorry about last time."

"There's no need to apologize. It was only natural you should get angry with me."

Roberto looked at him, bewildered.

"Why?"

"Why do you think it happened?"

"I don't know. At that particular moment I was really angry with you. Afterwards it seemed absurd."

"It was quite normal."

"It seems strange to me."

"I agree with you, it may seem strange. But it's fine."

"I don't know what to talk about today."

"Let's not say anything for a while, then."

14

That was how the fifty minutes passed, with a lot of silence and a few words, in a suspended atmosphere. If he'd been asked, Roberto would not have been able to say if he was cheerful or sad, calm or restless, excited or depressed. He wouldn't have been able to say anything about himself. He was feeling things he couldn't give a name to. After a while it occurred to him that he was in the position of somebody who has complicated emotions to explain but is forced to express himself in a language he barely knows. That seemed to him a good intuition and he tried to develop it, but before long he lost the thread and his thoughts floated away.

At the end of the session, the doctor told him that he would be away at a conference on Thursday, which meant they would see each other again in a week's time, next Monday.

Roberto registered the information but did not realize its full significance until he was going out into the street, where the rain was still coming down unrelentingly.

His movements around the city, his thoughts, his sleep, his meals, the television, the computer, smoking, drinking, exercising, washing, cooking, shopping – everything revolved around those two fixed times: five o'clock on Monday and five o'clock on Thursday.

The doctor's conference shifted the centre of gravity and produced a kind of landslide in Roberto's consciousness.

Walking in the rain, with the umbrella not really protecting him and the water soaking him to the skin, he was hit by a distressing awareness of the indistinct time opening in front of him. A sea as flat as oil, an infinite, deserted expanse, without terra firma on the horizon.

The week passed with gluey slowness, marked by a constant dull headache which was resistant to pills.

Roberto moved laboriously – as if having to drag a weight heavier than that of his own body – through a succession of identical days strung together.

He woke up early in the morning and went to sleep late at night. He walked obsessively throughout the city in the rain, which lasted a long time, most of the week, almost without interruption. Dripping wet, he would stop to eat in rotisseries and shabby restaurants hidden away on the extreme edge of the city, places he wouldn't have been able to find again an hour later. He smoked damp cigarettes in the precarious shelter of doorways or arcades. A couple of times he thought he saw faces he knew, but he had no idea who they were and had no desire to find out. Both times he looked away and moved on quickly, almost furtively.

On Sunday, the headache stopped.

On Monday morning, Roberto emerged from the dark, muddy pool he had been wading through all week.

Giacomo

I made the compilation. It wasn't easy to choose the songs and it took me several days, partly because I thought there shouldn't be too many of them, but above all I couldn't risk putting in stuff she wouldn't like. In other words, I had to play it safe.

In the end I chose six songs: "Time Is on My Side" by the Rolling Stones, "Everybody Hurts" by REM, "Tunnel of Love" by Dire Straits, "Don't Stop Me Now" by Queen, "With or Without You" by U2 and "Stairway to Heaven" by Led Zeppelin, which is my favourite song, because it reminds me of something beautiful, even though I can't remember what.

I also thought of giving the collection a title, but the ones I thought of didn't seem appropriate. In fact, they made me want to puke. Stuff like: *Songs for Ginevra* or *Giacomo's Selection* or other soppy things that make me ashamed just to write them in this diary.

In the end I gave up on the title, put the memory stick in my rucksack and carried it back and forth from home to school for a week without finding the opportunity or the courage to give it to her. Then she was away, and for two days now she hasn't been to school. I thought of phoning her, but I don't have her mobile number, and even if I had it there's no guarantee I'd find the courage to call her.

Last night, after hesitating for at least an hour, I asked her to be my friend on Facebook. Let's see what happens.

* * *

I had a nightmare, which hadn't happened to me for a while.

I was sitting on my bed, sure that I was wide awake, when I heard the rustle of wings. I was about to switch on the light but then, in the semi-darkness, I saw a pigeon perched on the lamp, looking at me.

Immediately after that, I saw two more of them on the floor, next to the bed. No, there weren't just two, there were more. Five, or maybe six or seven, or maybe ten. Or maybe twenty. Now they were all around, on the bedside table, on the desk, on the chair, even on the bed. The room was full of pigeons, and from somewhere I couldn't see others kept coming in. They were on the wardrobe, on the ceiling light, on the football. And now they were all looking at me. All grey, which in the darkness seemed black, all with the same stupid hostile nasty pigeon eyes.

But none of them moved.

They were too still, I thought, and so, making an effort to overcome my disgust, I reached out my hand to one of them that was on the bedside table. I touched it with one finger but it didn't move. I touched another and that one didn't move either.

Then I tried touching the third one, but a bit harder, and it fell to the floor, making a noise like a paper ball or a piece of cardboard. I tried to push another one and that one also fell, without giving any signs of life. Then, even though it really made me want to puke, I tried picking one up. I took it cautiously between my index finger and my thumb, and at that moment I understood.

It wasn't alive.

It was stuffed.

They were all stuffed, and as I was holding the one I had picked up between my fingers I heard a rustling spreading from the room. It didn't come from any place in particular.

The pigeons started falling, one after the other, a whole volley of them. A heavy shower of stuffed pigeons. It was really disgusting.

I shielded my head with my hands, making an effort not to scream, and stayed like that for all the time it lasted. Then, when the shower was over, I looked around, checked the floor and the bed.

There was nothing there, because I had woken up.

15

He was just getting ready to go out when his mobile phone rang. That was something that happened so rarely that at first Roberto didn't realize the sound had anything to do with him.

"Hello."

"Hi, it's Emma."

"Emma, hi."

"I remembered you'd written your telephone number in the book."

"Yes, it was inside the cover," Roberto replied, and a fraction of a second later felt like an idiot. If she was phoning him, that obviously meant she'd found the number.

"The book, yes. It's very good, thank you. Reading it brought back lots of memories."

At that moment it struck Roberto that Emma should have been at the doctor's office at this hour.

"Aren't you at the doctor's?"

"Actually, no. I couldn't go today. And I won't be going on Mondays any more, because... Well, it's not important, something to do with work. Anyway, I've changed days."

"Oh, so our date is cancelled?" He tried to give his voice a light tone, but the thought going through his brain was: if she had changed the day of her session, it was likely they'd never meet again.

"That's why I'm phoning you. As if we'd had a real date. I know it may seem ridiculous, but I thought that if you didn't see me you might get worried."

Then she paused, and in those moments of silence it seemed to Roberto that he could hear the frantic murmur of thoughts running out of control.

"It's true. If I hadn't seen you today I'd have got worried. Thank you."

Silence, heavy with unexpressed intentions. Each was aware of the other being about to speak and was waiting.

"Maybe —"

"I was thinking —"

"I'm sorry, carry on."

"No, you first."

"If you're not too busy tonight, maybe we could have a bite to eat or go for a drink. Tonight." He said *tonight* twice, although he couldn't have said why. And as he finished speaking, he was already regretting what he had said. What did he know about her, apart from what he had discovered on the Internet? She might be married – she didn't wear a wedding ring; come to think of it, she didn't wear any ring at all: that was his old attention to detail coming out – she might be with someone, she might have had no intention of seeing him and the phone call had been simply the impulsive act of an unstable person.

"Obviously if you can't or you don't feel like it, no problem," he said hastily. "I don't mean to be intrusive, I just wanted to say it."

She hesitated for a few seconds.

"I don't have much time. But maybe a drink would be fine. We'd have to meet near my place."

"Of course. Tell me where you live and I'll come there."

"I'm in the Via Panisperna. We could meet at Santa Maria dei Monti, there's a bar with tables in front… It's almost hot today, maybe we could sit outside."

Roberto did not reply. Santa Maria dei Monti was no more than two hundred yards from where he lived.

"Are you still there?"

"No, I mean yes, I'm sorry, something came into my head – it happens sometimes – and I got distracted. Santa Maria dei Monti would be perfect, I know the bar. What time shall we meet?"

"Maybe you're a long way away and it's hard for you to get to Monti, but I can't get away, I'm sorry."

"Monti really isn't a problem for me. Shall we say eight o'clock?"

"Yes, eight o'clock's fine," and then, after a brief hesitation: "I'm sorry..."

"Yes?"

"I warn you I'm about to make a fool of myself again, but I never listen to names when I make someone's acquaintance..."

"Neither do I."

"... and I didn't hear yours. I'm sorry."

"Roberto."

"Roberto. You could have written the name next to the phone number. That way you would have spared me the embarrassment of asking you."

"You're right, it's my fault. Tonight I'll let you have my full particulars and even leave you a photocopy of my ID, for all eventualities."

Laughter.

"Good idea, then I can check you're really a carabiniere. See you tonight, then."

"See you at eight."

16

He was feverish with excitement. He thought of calling the doctor's office, saying something had happened and he'd have to cancel that afternoon's appointment. He dismissed the idea almost immediately. He left home and ran most of the way, in order not to be overcome by the mental pins and needles that had taken hold of him after Emma's phone call.

Towards the end of the session – it had slipped away like a pleasant chat between two strangers in a railway carriage – the doctor asked him if everything was all right. Roberto said yes, everything was fine, but he had to excuse him if he was a bit distracted, for some days now he had been surprised by his own reactions, he didn't really know what to expect from himself, and now he really had to dash because he had an appointment this evening, sorry again, see you on Thursday.

As he left, he could feel the doctor's penetrating gaze on him, and told himself that by Thursday he would have to find an explanation for his behaviour.

* * *

After his shower he looked at himself in the mirror and realized that he had a paunch. Of course he'd known that for some time. Years and years of bad food and copious amounts of alcohol in different places around the world don't pass without leaving their mark.

But even though he'd known, it was only now that he became fully aware of it. In other words, that he *saw* it. He stood side on to the mirror, then again facing it. It occurred to him that he also needed to see himself from the back, but he didn't have a second mirror and so he couldn't. He tried to hold his breath. Then he contracted his abdominal muscles – which he definitely had, partly because he had been exercising again for a while. But equally definitely, they weren't visible. Many years earlier, he told himself, his abdominals had been like those you saw in commercials for swimming costumes. Now, they most certainly weren't. When had they started to disappear beneath a growing layer of fat? He didn't know. The years he'd spent living that absurd life were enveloped in a thin but distressing layer of fog. He knew he had been to Madrid, Geneva, London, Marseilles, Bogotá, Caracas, New York, Miami and lots of other places, but he couldn't put the memories of all those journeys, all those airports, all those hotels, all those meetings, all those lunches and banquets into any kind of order. Or all those women. Yes, that was another worrying thing. He couldn't remember the names, or even the faces, of many of the women. He remembered their bodies and in some cases even their smells. But not their faces or their names.

All right, he told himself. Best to stop right there and finish getting ready.

He realized he did not even have one bottle of cologne at home. I'll have to buy one, he promised himself, while starting to think about what to wear. This immediately produced a kind of mental paralysis, a sense of panic. How long was it since he'd last been shopping for clothes? All the clothes he had were old and – he thought, feeling embarrassed – rather pitiful. His apartment, too, was scruffy and pitiful. He was dismayed at the thought that Emma might come in here, see where he lived, and find out who he was, who he really was.

111

Then, beneath heaps of washed but unironed shirts, T-shirts, odd socks, pants with the elastic stretched and a few long-unworn ties, he unearthed, as if by a miracle, a new shirt, still in its plastic packaging. He unwrapped the shirt and put it on, then slipped on a pair of jeans – jeans are always more or less the same even if you've had them for quite some time – and finally took out the most presentable jacket he had in the wardrobe: the top part of a suit he'd had for years but had only worn two or maybe three times.

He felt better. He pulled in his belly and straightened his back, and it seemed to him he was not as run-down as he had thought just a while earlier. He made a few more grimaces to try and bring a little colour and expression to his face.

As he went out he decided that as soon as they met he would tell her they were neighbours, to avoid misunderstandings that might become unpleasant.

As he was early, he walked slowly and got to the Piazza della Madonna dei Monti at five to eight. That gave him a reassuring sense of control and a little leap of joy. There was a carefree atmosphere, the sense of slightly euphoric anticipation typical of the first evenings of spring. A few young people sat laughing on the steps of the fountain, two overweight elderly ladies were chatting in Roman dialect, a man was collecting, with a little shovel and bag, what his dog had just deposited on the cobbles.

Roberto sat down at an outside table and continued to look around with the same curiosity and a vague sense of surprise, as if this were the first time he had been to this square.

Emma arrived five minutes late. She, too, was dressed in a springlike way. Jeans, white shirt, jacket, leather bag over her shoulder, raincoat over her arm.

"I'm sorry, I hate being late," she said, sitting down with a friendly smile and spreading around her that perfume which already seemed familiar to Roberto.

"Only five minutes."

"Six minutes," she said, looking at her watch. "You know, up until a few years ago I made it a rule always to arrive really late. Twenty minutes, even half an hour sometimes. Then the subject came up at our doctor's and he explained what it means."

"What does it mean?"

"It's a way of exercising power. A kind of bullying, a concealed abuse of authority. Anyway, something I really didn't like. When he told me that, I said I thought that was nonsense, you can't attribute a pathological explanation to everything, the reason I arrived late was because I always had too much to do and couldn't get through it, things like that. I was quite unpleasant in the way I replied, quite aggressive. Which happened often at the beginning."

"And what did he say?"

"He smiled, which made me even more nervous, and then said that when I felt like it I should ask myself why the subject bothered me so much. And when I felt like it I could tell him what the result of my reflection had been."

"Yes, I can almost picture him and hear his voice."

"And of course he was right. I'd got upset because he was right. He'd caught me out, as on so many other occasions. It took me a while to tell him that, but since then I've started to pay attention to this thing about arriving late. It happens much less now, but some habits are difficult to change completely. When it does happen, when I arrive even just a few minutes late, I always apologize. I'm still a convalescent. I brought you this."

"What is it?" Roberto asked.

"*I Am a Bird Now* by Antony and the Johnsons. Do you know it?"

"No, but I don't really know much about music."

"I was just leaving and then I thought I'd like to give you

113

something of mine, seeing that I liked your book so much. So I grabbed this. Do you mind second-hand?"

Receiving a gift was something that hadn't happened to him for some time, and Roberto realized he didn't know how to react. He had to make an effort just to say thank you and smile. Then he took the CD and looked at the cover. At that moment the waitress arrived. Emma ordered a light Aperol spritz. Roberto said the same thing would be fine for him.

"I live in the Via Panisperna... Oh, sorry, I already told you that. Do you know the area?"

"Yes, I live here."

"How do you mean?"

"I'm in the Via del Boschetto."

"Just round the corner?"

"Yes."

"No way. Why didn't you tell me that before?"

"When you told me you lived around here I was so surprised that I didn't have the presence of mind to tell you."

"Look at you. We must have passed each other dozens of times."

She sighed, smiled, shook her head.

"Do you have a cigarette?"

"Do you smoke?" he asked, in a slightly surprised tone.

"Other people's cigarettes. I never buy my own, or else I'd smoke a packet a day."

Roberto took out a packet of red Dianas and a lighter, cursing himself for not having thought of buying more.

"These are all I have. They're not exactly ladies' cigarettes."

She ignored the remark, took the packet and lighter, lit a cigarette and smoked half of it greedily, without saying a word. The waitress arrived and placed their drinks on the table, along with peanuts and crisps.

"How long have you been living around here?"

"It was my mother's apartment. I lived there with her from the age of sixteen to the age of nineteen. Then I left for the Carabinieri's officers' training academy. Twenty-five, twenty-six years went by and, just under two years ago, I came back to live here."

"With your mother?"

"No, she died…" Roberto stopped, completely at a loss. He couldn't remember when his mother had died. He had to make a great effort to go back first to the year, then to the month, finally to the day. It was like climbing up a wall without any handholds.

"My mother died almost five years ago. The apartment was empty until I came, after… certain things changed in my job." He had been about to tell her that before, for many years, he had lived in safe houses, service accommodation, hotels, apartment blocks. He had been about to add that he had never had a real home of his own in his life, apart from the years in California. He had been about to do so, but then he told himself that now was not the time, not yet at least.

"I've also been here for about two years," she said. "No, maybe a bit longer, nearly three. But I actually grew up here. Right now I'm living in the same building where my parents live. They have two apartments. They've given me one, and I live there with my son."

She had speeded up at the end of the sentence, as if she wanted to be sure she got everything in, or as if to overcome her embarrassment.

"You have a child." The one you were expecting when you did that commercial for mineral water, he thought, without saying it.

"When he hears someone call him a child he gets really angry: he's eleven, almost twelve."

"Almost twelve," Roberto repeated in a low voice and a slightly absent tone. He was silent for a few seconds and then

115

appeared to rouse himself, as if a thought had crossed his mind and then slipped away.

"And where did you live up to the age of sixteen?"

"In California. That's where I was born."

He paused.

"My father was American. When he died, my mother and I left."

"You mean you have dual personality… Sorry, I meant dual nationality."

Roberto burst out laughing, and it struck him that he hadn't laughed like that for quite some time.

"I think dual personality is an excellent definition. And yes, I do have dual nationality."

"I'm sorry, I say the most awful rubbish, I don't know how it happens."

"But that's exactly how it is, you don't have to apologize. In fact, maybe dual personality is an underestimate. There are a lot more than two."

"Roberto. That is your name?"

"Yes."

"Roberto, there's something I think I ought to say."

"Go on."

"I don't think I'm ready for a sexual relationship. I want to avoid misunderstandings and I don't want to offend you in any way."

"Well, you certainly don't beat about the bush."

"I like you. What I'm going to say may seem absurd, but in the few times we've met, I've somehow grown fond of you. That's why I want to avoid misunderstandings. My life is still a mess, I'm trying to pull myself out of the disasters of the past, and there are a whole lot of things I'm not ready for."

She took another cigarette from the packet that still lay on the table.

"I'm talking like a character in a bad film."

"That's all right, I mostly watch bad films. And anyway, there are a lot of things I'm not ready for either. Including sex, since you've mentioned the subject. I really hadn't thought our meeting like this would lead to anything sexual."

Was it true? Roberto didn't actually know. Maybe it was true, or maybe he said that to overcome his embarrassment, and maybe also to give her a small, harmless lesson. You're not ready for sex (meaning: with me, seeing that I'm the one with you right now), well, neither am I (meaning: with you, seeing that you're the one with me right now).

She looked at him, somewhat surprised. She played with her cigarette. Then she lit it. Then she asked him why he didn't have one too. Roberto replied that he didn't feel like one right now. She seemed to be about to add something but then gave up. There was a slight tension between the two of them. Nothing to get alarmed about, but definitely there.

"You do know I'm a psychiatric patient?"

"So am I."

"And as a good psychiatric patient, having just informed you that I'm not ready for a sexual relationship, I was rather annoyed to hear you say that it was the same for you. *I* may have the right not to have sexual intentions towards a man but it doesn't have to be mutual, does it?"

He looked at her through half-closed eyes.

"Don't give me that look," she said with a smile. "You can't say something like that, to a woman in general, and an actress in particular. Or even an ex-actress. We're fragile creatures. We need to be treated gently."

She hesitated, but it was clearly an intentional pause. Roberto mustn't say anything, just wait.

"We all worry about other people's judgement to some extent, we all seek approval. That's normal. The problem arises – and for actors it arises very easily – when the search for approval becomes a kind of addiction. And the next stage is paranoia."

117

"How do you mean?"

"You start to divide the world into those who approve of you, love you, admire you, think you're wonderful, and everybody else. In other words the bad guys, who, in some obscure way, all agree among themselves."

She broke off abruptly.

"All right, I have an actress's paranoia, even though I'm not an actress any more. I'm really quite pathetic."

"Is that why you started seeing the doctor?"

She looked at him as if she did not understand. As if the question had been formulated in another language. Then she relaxed. She made an almost amused face, although with a remote hint of dismay.

"Did I start seeing the doctor because of my actress's paranoia? No, that would have been too sophisticated a reason. And it certainly wouldn't be enough to justify spending the money I've spent and am still spending on him. The only reason I started seeing the doctor was because my life had fallen to pieces. Just a little thing like that."

Roberto would have liked to reply that this meant they'd both started seeing the doctor for the same reason. He didn't do so, because he wasn't sure he'd find the right tone. She said that smoking a third cigarette was excessive, that it would be better to avoid it. Then, with perfect consistency, she lit one. She blew out the smoke and emptied her glass.

"Part of me is telling me to drop this, another part has a great desire to tell you everything. Can we drink something a little more interesting? I don't know, a fifteen-percent Primitivo from Apulia? Shall we get them to bring us something to eat?"

He looked at her without formulating the question, although it must have been quite clear on his face. So clear that she was immediately aware of it.

"Now you must be thinking I told you I didn't have much time."

"You did tell me that."

"I wanted to keep a way out open. Who is this man, after all? Someone I met by chance, and at the psychiatrist's to boot. Maybe I'll be bored after just ten minutes. Maybe he's got the wrong idea about me – after all, he's crazy like me, like everybody who sees the doctor. Maybe he's a pervert, maybe he has homicidal tendencies, maybe he's a potential rapist, whatever. In other words, I wanted to be free to run away at any moment, without any hassle."

"So what happened?"

"What happened is that I haven't felt like running away. I like the way you listen. It makes me want to talk. I suppose that means you're good at your job."

What job? He didn't have a job any more. He still drew a marshal's salary while on extended leave for health reasons, but a job – something he knew, something he was able to do – he no longer had. When the maximum period of leave for health reasons was over, he would have to come to a decision. Either go back, maybe in command of a station like the one he'd happened to land up in at the beginning of his career, dealing with petty disputes between neighbours, people driving without a licence, and thefts of car radios. Did anyone still steal car radios? No, not any more. So not even that.

Or else leave. That might be the best solution. Was he entitled to a pension? He had never wondered about that, maybe because the question had never crossed his mind until that moment, as he was talking to her. Maybe he was entitled to a disability pension even before he reached the age limit. Or maybe, he seemed to recall, with at least twenty years of service, you had a right to a pension even though you had to wait until you were a certain age. A certain age, what a horrible expression. Where could he go to find out what it was, that certain age when he would get his pension?

Her voice revived him.

"Hey, are you there?"

"I'm sorry. You mentioned my job and I started thinking. I got distracted."

"You really did. You looked as if you were somewhere else entirely."

"Then let's sort out the rest of the evening. If we want a glass of wine and something to eat, it might be better to go to a restaurant. Do you have any preferences?"

"You bet I do," she said with a smile. She was suddenly like a little girl, and he could feel his heart breaking and crumbling and becoming something insubstantial. "It's been ages since I last ate Indian. There's an Indian restaurant right near here that I used to like a lot. I don't know if it's still as good as it was. But we could try it, if that's OK with you?"

Giacomo

Ginevra hasn't been back to school – she's been absent for three days now – and hasn't even replied to my friendship request on Facebook. Nobody knows why she's away and I'm starting to get worried.

I think that's why I woke up very early today and couldn't get back to sleep. I couldn't just stay in bed so I got up and started writing down last night's dream, to pass the time and get over my nervousness.

I fell asleep reading (my mother must have come in to turn off the light) and soon afterwards found myself back in the park. Scott wasn't there, and unlike the other times the sky was quite cloudy, the air was cooler, almost cold, and the grass seemed taller. I looked around, and in the middle of the lawn I saw Ginevra. I waved to her but she didn't respond; she turned and walked quickly away.

I started going after her, quite fast, but however fast I went I couldn't catch up with her. The quicker I went, the greater the distance between us. I tried to start running, but my legs seemed really heavy, I felt as if I was moving in slow motion, and after a while I slipped and fell. Ginevra was getting further and further away, and growing smaller and smaller, until she completely disappeared into the grass.

I sat down on the ground, discouraged. I felt very alone and very unhappy.

Everything all right, chief?

I turned and saw Scott trotting towards me.

"Scott. Thank goodness you're here. Where have you been?"

Hey, chief, you look terrible. What's happened?

It didn't strike me at the time, but Scott is very good at not answering questions when he doesn't want to.

"Ginevra was here. I waved to her and she didn't wave back. I tried to go to her and she got away."

Scott looked at me with an expression I couldn't figure out.

"What's happening, Scott? Ginevra hasn't been to school for days, and now that I meet her here she runs away."

I don't know, chief, but I get the feeling something's wrong on the other side.

"What do you mean?"

The other side is when you're awake, chief, you know. But that's a territory I don't know much about.

Even though I was worried and sad about Ginevra, these words of Scott reminded me of things I'd been wanting to ask him for a while.

"Do you remember the first time we met, Scott?"

How could I ever forget, chief?

"You remember who was with me…"

Your father.

Your father.

I don't think anyone's ever said those two words to me. Or at least I don't remember. The few times when Mum talks about my father she says *your dad*, and with Grandma and Grandpa it's the same. When I think about my father I almost always use the word *father*, but hearing someone else use it, I don't know, it just gives me the idea that it's true and not something that only exists in my memory and my imagination.

Your dad isn't a bad expression, not at all. But – it's difficult to explain – it gives me the idea of a relationship between a

122

man and a child. In other words, the only thing there's ever been between him and me, which is over for ever.

"Why did he leave and never come back?"

As I was finishing the sentence I realized I wasn't sure if I was talking about the first dream where I met Scott or about when my father left home and never came back. And I realized I was angry – very angry – with him, because he had gone and never come back. In the real world, or in the dream, or in both.

Scott said nothing and continued looking at me with the same serious expression as before.

"You know my father was a writer?"

Yes chief, your father and I know each other well.

"If you know each other well, why don't you ever let me see him? I really need to talk to him."

Your father is always around here somewhere, even though you can't always see him. There are things he has to tell you, but he doesn't know how.

"What does he have to tell me?"

Now Scott didn't just seem serious, he seemed sad and even uncertain – which was unlike him – about what to do.

"What does my father have to tell me, Scott?"

He sighed and maybe made up his mind to reply. But at that precise moment I woke up. I tried to get to sleep again and go back into the dream to hear that reply, but it was impossible.

It's always impossible.

17

When the moment came to drink the Cabernet they had ordered and poured in their glasses, Roberto hesitated for a moment, and Emma noticed.

"You're not teetotal, are you? No, you can't be, you had a spritz."

"It's just that I'm still on medication and apparently you have to be careful not to mix it with alcohol. I've already had one drink… But it's all right, there's no problem, I'll drink the wine but won't take any medication tonight. The doctor said I can, from time to time. Even though I've never done it before, and to be honest the idea makes me a bit nervous. Well, if the worst comes to the worst, I won't sleep tonight."

"Still on medication? How long have you been seeing the doctor?"

"I've been going since…"

Again that unpleasant sensation of not being able to locate things in time. How long had he been seeing the doctor? He floundered, as he had when he'd been trying to remember the year his mother had died.

He had started seeing the doctor just after the end of summer.

Yes, in September. It was April now, which made seven months, give or take.

"Seven months, more or less."

And what day is today? Monday, of course, because he'd been to the doctor's and should have met Emma there, but she hadn't gone. It seemed to him as if it wasn't just a few hours that had passed since he'd been getting ready to go out, but days, quite a few days in fact. The feeling was so strong that Roberto wondered if it actually had been several days and he was getting confused, caught irreparably now in this personal trap of time. But, to go back to the question, what day was it in April? What date?

Again that sense of panic, that impression of being lost in unknown territory. A place where monstrous entities might be hiding behind familiar everyday objects. Entities that could jump on you or eat you up. He couldn't reconstruct what day it was – it must be round about the middle of April – and thought of looking at his mobile. But he would have had to take it out of his pocket and actually look at it, and that struck him as impolite and somehow cowardly. Tomorrow he would buy a calendar and make a note of what day it was, every day. And little by little he would reconstruct the chronology of the past few months, and then of the past few years, of his life.

"What day is today?"

"Monday, 18 April. Why?"

"Every now and again I get mixed up. And yes, I am taking various medications."

"I stopped taking the heavy stuff a few months ago. I still take a dozen drops of Minias in the evening, though. The doctor says that's all right, that it's important to sleep and that a few drops of tranquillizer never hurt anybody."

Roberto was a little surprised by this light, cheerful way of dealing with the subject. In the end he raised his glass in a toast, Emma responded, and they drank. She was looking at him and he couldn't interpret her expression but he liked it.

Everything came at the same time: plates and bowls with rice, naan bread, chicken tikka masala, lamb curry, vegetables.

Emma flung herself on the food as if just coming off a long fast, and for about ten minutes they did not talk much.

They emerged from silence as they were waiting for dessert.

"So, to sum up: you said you don't act any more?"

"I suppose you'd like to know what I do."

"If that isn't confidential information."

"I'm a shop assistant." She said it with a slight but perceptible note of aggressiveness in her voice.

"I'm sorry?"

"My friends all get angry when I say that. They say it's a way to feel sorry for myself and that I'm not a shop assistant. Let's say I'm a high-class shop assistant, but I'm still a shop assistant."

"Maybe you should give me a few more clues."

"When I realized I couldn't and didn't want to be an actress any more, I started looking for a completely different kind of job. The problem was that there wasn't anything I knew how to do. There still isn't. Apart from singing a bit, and producers aren't exactly queuing to sign me up for a record deal. Anyway, I had to find something suitable for someone who doesn't know how to do anything. I put the word out and, after a few ridiculous propositions, a friend called me. Actually he was a friend of a friend, and he told me he was about to open a kind of art gallery, or rather a cross between an art gallery and a high-class furniture shop. Paintings, sculpture, furniture, objects. Would I be interested in working there? Of course I would, but I wasn't any kind of expert, either about art or about furniture. High-class or otherwise."

"What did he say to that?"

"He's a self-made man. A good man in his way, but not exactly sophisticated. He said he didn't want me for my expertise. He said, and here I quote, that I was dishy, I had a *fairly* well-known face and knew how to deal with people."

"And what did you say?"

"Overcoming my annoyance at that bit about being *fairly* well-known, I told him we could talk about it. We met and, to cut a long story short, I agreed. And I made the right decision. It isn't the life I'd dreamed about when I was studying to be an actress, but the work isn't hard, and I get to meet interesting people in pleasant surroundings. The wages are nothing to write home about, but I've lowered my standards compared with the past. And I don't have to ask my parents for money to provide for my son, to pay the doctor, to go to the cinema or a few concerts. But I never go to the theatre. I still don't think I can bear being in the audience and not up there on the stage."

"The theatre was your passion?"

"It was my passion. I did quite a bit of it, I even played Viola in *Twelfth Night*, but let's be honest about it: I was very average as an actress. And when I was a little girl and dreamed about being an actress, I didn't dream about being *average*. For years I looked for and found all kinds of explanations for why I was so average. The most obvious one only became clear to me when I stopped, or rather some time after I'd stopped: I just wasn't talented enough."

Roberto noticed at that moment that the waiter had a slight limp and produced a kind of syncopated tapping, that there was music in the background, and that the door of the restaurant made an unpleasant squeaking sound when it opened and closed. It was as if a muffler had been taken off the surrounding sounds.

"Now you're wondering why I stopped. Am I wrong?"

"No, you aren't wrong."

"Maybe I'll tell you next time. If we go too fast we risk hurting ourselves."

Hurting ourselves. Hurting yourself. Let's not hurt ourselves. Don't hurt yourselves, children. I hurt myself, mummy. It hurts. What did I do wrong to hurt myself, daddy? Was I bad?

Daddy.

Bad.

Bad.

Words. Fragments of glass, cutting.

Roberto spoke slowly, choosing with care the few elementary words of the question. Cautiously, as if he were walking on a wire or handling sharp, dangerous objects.

"What year is your son in?"

"He's in middle school, but he's a year ahead. He'll be twelve in May. Now they say we ought to let them play longer, that it isn't a good idea to send them to school too early. At the time, though, they told me he was so good, so precocious, it was a pity not to let him gain a year. If I could do it all over again, I'd make him go to school normally. What about you? Do you have a wife, children? Tell me about your life."

Again the tapping of the limping waiter. Much louder than before. Very loud. Too loud. Except that now the waiter was nowhere near them. Pins and needles. Nerves on edge. Elusive reflexes. Are you mad? Maybe, but basically we all are. A wife, no, certainly not. Children? Certainly not. Certainly not. Certainly not.

"No. I've never been married." He heard his own voice. It came from God knows where and had an unusual solidity. Maybe I came close to it, he thought of saying, just to add something. But he didn't want to.

"And you told me you're a carabiniere."

"Yes."

"But something like a captain, an officer?"

"I'm a marshal."

"Wow, that's impressive," she said with an ironic smile. The same one, it seemed to Roberto, that she'd had in that commercial for condoms. "Of course, when I hear the word *marshal* I think of a man in a rather ridiculous uniform, with a paunch and a big moustache."

He felt a slight pang of annoyance over the *rather ridiculous uniform*. But that brought him back to the table and the conversation, which was a good thing.

"The marshal in charge of the station where I had my first posting was pretty much like that."

"And what exactly do you do, as a carabiniere?"

He tried to think of an answer as quickly as possible. Tell the truth. Tell a pack of lies. Mix truth and lies. In other words, what he had always done.

"Now, to tell the truth, nothing. I'm on leave for health reasons. I don't know where they'll put me when I go back. If I go back."

"Because you went mad?" The same smile as before.

"Because they noticed. I was mad before, but I was better at hiding it." That had come out well.

"And before they noticed?"

For a few seconds Roberto was again aware of a shift in the axis of reality in this conversation. The question – before they noticed? – even though part of their humorous banter, seemed to him a serious and pertinent one. It fact, it *was* serious and pertinent. Emma knew something about him and was calling him to account. She knew some of the things he had done, things he had never admitted to anyone, not even the doctor. Maybe she also knew some of the things he hadn't had the courage to confess even to himself. Roberto wavered in fear before escaping that wave of folly and managing to respond. Then the coordinates of the conversation returned to normality.

"I was in a special operations group, and worked undercover for many years."

"You mean you infiltrated gangs, that kind of thing?"

"Yes, that's exactly it. Strictly speaking, I shouldn't really talk about it, but I don't suppose you have many acquaintances who are international cocaine traffickers. And besides, I've finished with that work for ever. Even if they take me back."

"Why have you finished with it for ever? Is it something to do with the problems that brought you to the doctor?"

"I'd say so." He was behaving himself. He wasn't telling lies. He was moving cautiously along the thin ridge separating truth from lies.

They fell silent. Roberto looked Emma in the face, following the line of her cheek all the way from her cheekbone to her mouth.

She drank some wine and wiped a drop from her lips with the edge of her napkin.

"You don't have to answer. I told you I wasn't ready to talk about my story; I assume it's the same for you."

"It's hard to talk about undercover work. It's all about playing a part, a role. The problem is, you have to play it for a long time, for months, sometimes even years. The people you spend most of your time with – the criminals – are the same people you're going to have arrested. They think of you as a colleague and sometimes a friend, but you're working to put them in prison. It's easy to lose your balance when you live like that for a long time."

Good. No lies. All true, but without specific facts, keeping away from sharp corners, avoiding touching the points that made him scream with pain.

"In a way, you were an actor too."

Roberto reflected on the exact significance of that phrase.

"Yes," he said at last. "In a way, I was an actor too."

"Tell me some stories about your work. I'm really curious."

Roberto was about to say that it was better if he didn't, that now wasn't the time, that it was all in the past and wasn't worth dredging up. Instead he said "all right" and started talking.

"It was the early Nineties, I was working in Milan in those days. I was doing normal detective work, no undercover operations. We had to do an ambient."

"What does that mean?"

"A ambient intercept. It means we had to bug a guy's home."

"Why?"

"He was a big-time ecstasy dealer. When you have to do an ambient, you always have the same problem. How to get into the guy's apartment, or office, or warehouse, or car, and plant the bugs without him noticing. At that time we often used a trick that's now been discontinued. In the sense that after a while word got out and nobody fell for it any more."

"What trick?"

"We'd get in touch with the phone company and ask them to block the line, the person would call for help, we'd show up dressed as engineers, and use the pretext of checking to find out the cause of the breakdown to plant the bug. We'd install it in the phone because it was easier to hide it there and activate it, but it would pick up everything, not just phone calls."

"You really did things like that?" she said, smiling and leaning forward across the table.

Roberto nodded and also smiled.

* * *

The line was blocked. The dealer asked for assistance. A few hours later Roberto and a colleague showed up at his apartment with their uniforms and their phone company badges.

"Good day to you, signore, is it you who called for technical assistance?"

He was a plump man in a tight-fitting sweat suit, with full lips, not much hair, small, suspicious eyes, and the air of someone confident he can handle every situation. He lived in a two-roomed apartment filled with cheap furniture. There was a smell of mustiness, cigarettes and sweat.

"I called, yes. This fucking phone has been dead since this morning."

The other carabiniere – his name was Filomeno, not a name

you'd forget in a hurry – picked up the phone, tried to dial a number, unscrewed the receiver, pretended to examine the contents, and took apart the socket. He was waiting for the right moment to install the bug, but the dealer hadn't taken his eyes off him.

"You don't think I'm being bugged, do you?" the dealer asked at a certain point, while the two carabinieri were still pretending to be busy with their technical operations.

We'd like to bug you, Roberto thought, but if you don't do something else for a few seconds we can't put the fucking bug in. It was at that moment that the idea came to him. "It's possible," he said circumspectly.

He could feel the other carabiniere's eyes on him: he must be wondering if his colleague had gone mad.

"And how can I find out?"

Roberto looked at him with the expression of someone making up his mind if he can trust the person he is talking to.

"Usually you can't, but…"

"But?"

"In theory we could check. It's illegal, though, and very risky."

"I could pay you."

Roberto let a few more seconds pass, as if he were weighing up the pros and cons.

"How much?" asked the other carabiniere, who by now had cottoned on to the game.

"150,000 now and 150,000 when you give me the answer."

Roberto shook his head.

"300,000 to be split between the two of us? To risk prison? Don't even think about it."

"How much do you want?"

"500,000 now and 500,000 after we've checked."

The dealer looked first at Roberto, then at Filomeno, then again at Roberto.

"You've done this before, haven't you?" he said finally, in the

132

tone of someone who knows men and knows that everyone has a price. "This is how you supplement your income, isn't it?"

Then he went into his bedroom to get the money. By the time he came back, two minutes later, the bug had already been planted. Five hundred thousand lire in notes of various nominations – clearly the proceeds of his dealing – changed hands, later to be recorded as confiscated property. In the afternoon Roberto dropped by to give him the answer. The line was working again and he could rest easy: there weren't any bugs.

Not only could he rest easy, he could *talk* in peace to the customers who came to see him at home, Roberto thought as he left with another five hundred thousand lire in crumpled banknotes.

The rest of the investigation was easy. It only took two weeks of intercepts and a bit of physical surveillance to arrest the plump man in possession of a few thousand doses ready for sale in discotheques in the city and the province.

* * *

"I could listen to these stories for hours," Emma said when he had finished. "You liked doing that work, didn't you?"

More or less the same question as the doctor. Except that this time it didn't make him uncomfortable.

"Actually, investigative work can be quite boring. You spend hours listening to phone calls, transcribing conversations, watching the movements of someone who doesn't do a damn thing all day, or maybe scouring records to find out all you can about the suspects, which was the thing I personally hated the most. But then, of course, there are moments when you think you wouldn't like to do any other kind of job in the world."

And other moments when you wonder if it's all worth it. The sentence materialized in his head but did not transfer to his voice.

Emma covered her mouth to stifle a yawn.

"Maybe we should call it a night," Roberto said. "It's getting late."

"Oh, no, I'm sorry. I wasn't yawning out of boredom. I'm just a bit tired, that's all, but I really don't want to call it a night. How would you feel about going for a ride? Spring is here, let's take my motorbike and see a little of Rome by night."

"You ride a motorbike?"

"Only from time to time these days. I used to use it a lot more. There are loads of things I used to do and never do now, or hardly ever. But tonight, with this air, seems like the right time. What do you say?"

I had a great bike once too.

A really great bike it was. And I did some really stupid things with a group of idiots like me. We'd go out on the autostrada at night and take our bikes up to a hundred and twenty miles an hour, sometimes even faster. I also got into some crazy chases on my bike when I worked in robbery. I could have crashed at any moment during those rides or those chases. But it never crossed my mind. Ever. I wasn't afraid of anything. Death didn't exist.

But then I started to feel afraid of everything. I'd never thought about it so clearly as I did at that moment. I started to feel afraid of death just when I stopped caring about my life. I stopped riding a motorbike. I stopped doing a lot of things. When you ride a motorbike – the way I rode it – you're always very close to the edge. A moment before, you're all-powerful, invincible, a moment later you're a lifeless body, a broken doll, with your eyes open and your mouth half-open in surprise.

I had a great bike once too.

Roberto thought all these things simultaneously. He shuddered and took a deep breath.

"All right, let's go."

18

Emma came out of the garage on her bike, with her helmet already on her head. She had another one for Roberto, hanging from the handlebars.

"I hope it fits you," she said, pointing to it.

Roberto put on the helmet with a certain effort, got on, gripped the sides of the saddle, and smelled the aroma of Emma's hair. Then they set off.

Emma rode with confidence, communicating a sense of composure. She wasn't going fast but gave the impression she could do so at any moment and still keep control of the vehicle.

They sailed smoothly through the streets, and the bike, at that speed, was almost silent. It wove easily between the cars, rounded the bends, and on the darkest corners seemed to swallow the night in its headlight.

Every now and again, when they stopped at traffic lights, Emma would say something, but Roberto couldn't make out the words. He held on tight, looking at the streets as they passed by without recognizing them. He barely noticed, at a certain point, that they were crossing the Tiber, leaving the lights of Castel Sant'Angelo on their right. They stopped about ten minutes later and Roberto got off the bike with the feeling that it had been his first time. In a way it really was, he thought, looking around. They were on the Janiculum Hill.

The calm roar of the fountain. A smell of cut grass and unknown flowers. Not many cars. A reassuring blur of lights in the distance. A small pack of stray dogs walking slowly, calmly, following their leader into the gap beneath a flight of steps, to be swallowed up by the city glittering below.

Looking at the dogs, Roberto thought about all the sleepless hours he had spent walking the streets, smoking. Plenty of stray dogs then, along with seagulls, the last customers leaving late-night restaurants, policemen and carabinieri, street cleaners, vans carrying newspapers hot off the press, then the silence of the hour when there really is nobody about, then the first people emerging from their homes and running in the cold and dark, then the first people coming out to go to work, and then all the others, and then the day, when hiding is more difficult.

"Sorry, but is this a cliché?" she asked.

Roberto shook himself.

"Is what a cliché?"

"I don't know. Coming here…"

"I'm going to tell you something you won't believe."

"Go on."

"This is only the second time in my life that I've been here."

"You're right, I don't believe you. How is that possible?"

He shrugged. There were cities in the world where he had spent just a few weeks, but which he knew much better than Rome.

"Let me tell you something else."

"All right," she said, with the expression of someone embarking on a game that is likely to be full of surprises.

"I've never been inside the Coliseum and I've never visited the Forum. Actually, I've visited hardly any of the famous places in Rome."

"Are you joking?"

"No."

"That's not possible. People come from all over the world just to see those places. You live a few hundred yards away and you've never been there."

It didn't seem so important to Roberto. Or maybe it was, but he wasn't capable of distinguishing important things from those that were less so.

"That's quite unacceptable. I'll take you there one of these days. We'll take the bike one sunny Saturday afternoon and do *Roman Holiday* in reverse."

"Roman holiday? How do you mean?"

"The film with Audrey Hepburn and Gregory Peck. Don't tell me you've never seen it."

Roberto had never seen it, but knew vaguely what it was about and lied with a nonchalant gesture. Of course he had seen it, for heaven's sake, even though it was a long time ago and he could remember hardly anything about it.

As he told the lie, it struck him that he couldn't remember most of the films he had seen in his life. Was there a difference between never having seen a film, visited a place or read a book, and having seen it, visited it or read it and remembering nothing about it?

"And now that we've mentioned it: they say I look like Audrey Hepburn. I tend not to pay too much attention to that, but the fact that you haven't yet noticed does annoy me a bit."

Roberto looked at her and didn't see anything that reminded him of Audrey Hepburn. But he lied again and said yes, of course, how could he not have noticed, there was a definite resemblance.

"That used to make me so happy when I was a little girl. It seemed like a sign from fate, that I was predestined."

Emma's words hung in the air for a long time over the fountain and then were swallowed up by the noise of the water.

"Who's your son with right now?"

"His grandmother, who's always happy when I ask her to look after him. Actually, Giacomo's quite big now and I could leave him on his own, but I can't get used to the idea that he's growing up so quickly. In many ways he's much older than his age. The books he reads, the music he listens to, the things he writes. Even the things he says. When I can get him to speak."

"What do you mean?"

"He's a very quiet boy, very introverted. It isn't easy to talk to him."

She seemed about to add something, but at the last moment held back, as if an unexpected thought had stopped her in mid-flow. She made an impatient gesture with her hand.

"Anyway, I was telling you about my mother. She was pleased when I asked her to stay with Giacomo, because I almost never go out in the evening and she's worried about me, because I'm alone, I don't have a boyfriend, or a partner, whatever you want to call it. I don't think we ever stop worrying about our children. Sometimes the thought of that scares me. We want to protect them from everything, but we can't do that for ever."

We want to protect them.

Our children.

Dizziness.

Calm down. Everything's under control. Calm down.

Listen to her voice. Concentrate on her voice and breathe.

Calm down.

"Giacomo gets on well with his grandmother. Less with his grandfather. My mother's still young, my father's quite a bit older than her. They're both doctors – he's retired now and she's still working. He isn't ageing well. He was a handsome man – actually, he still is – and he can't bear the thought of old age. He cheated on her lots of times and she knew. I've often wondered why she stayed with him, and I've never found an answer. Or rather, I've found it and I don't like it, so I try not to think about it. Now the positions are reversed: she's the one who has someone else, a married man. She doesn't flaunt it, but she doesn't do anything to hide it either. She lies, but without worrying too much whether or not her lies are believable, without making too much of an effort not to be found out. Actually, I think my father knows all about it and just pretends he doesn't. Because he's afraid that if he says something she may leave him. She's kind to him, she takes care of him and they still sometimes go out together. But the whole power balance has changed, and now my father is the weaker of the two. Life can be pitiless."

From somewhere in the distance came two brief screams, almost moans.

"You know I'm astonished?"

"Why?"

"I've told you… some very private things. Why do I trust you?"

"I don't know," Roberto replied, with a shrug.

"Maybe I trust you because, despite appearances, you seem fragile. When you got on the bike I realized you were scared. Please don't take what I'm about to say in the wrong way, but I felt sorry for you."

"Was I scared?"

"Why, weren't you?"

Roberto would have liked to tell her about himself, but knew he wasn't capable.

And yet he was tired of feeling so alone and desperate and guilty.

Guilty.

We never stop worrying about our children.

We want to protect them from everything.

"The noise of the fountain's starting to get on my nerves. Shall we go somewhere quieter?"

Roberto made contact again, with difficulty.

"Yes, of course."

They put on their helmets, glided along in the darkness for a few hundred yards, and ended up sitting on a bench between the Garibaldi monument and the cannon.

"Can you give me another cigarette?"

Roberto took the packet from his jacket pocket and handed it to her.

They smoked calmly. The air was mild, as if spring were well advanced. Emma's story began suddenly, taking him by surprise.

"I got married because I was pregnant. He was a screenwriter."

She said a surname as if Roberto was sure to know it. But Roberto had never heard it before, or if he had ever chanced to hear it he had forgotten it.

"It was a mistake and I knew that perfectly well. There's a sentence by a writer – I can't remember who – that he loved to quote. It's something like this: 'Love means inventing the other person with all our imagination and all our strength, without yielding an inch to reality.' Unfortunately we'd already yielded several yards to reality when we discovered that we were about to have a baby. The most sensible thing to do would have been to keep the child but separate. The thing that everybody would have expected was for us to keep the child and continue living together, without being married. But he said maybe we should get married and I said yes. Without thinking. Or maybe I was thinking. Maybe I was thinking this would make things that weren't solid more solid. Or the opposite, thinking this was the best way to make sure things ended quickly."

Roberto remained silent. The words that came into his head all seemed stupid and banal.

Anyway – Emma continued – they got married, the child was born and they called him Giacomo. Three years later, she met someone else and they started seeing each other. In secret, of course, but it was obvious that sooner or later her husband would find out. And in fact he did, and wasn't well pleased. Quarrels, screaming and shouting, a pretence of fair play, just make up your mind, if you want me to I'll leave, don't be so theatrical, that's too easy, these things happen to everyone, maybe it's even happened to you, sorry to disappoint you but no, it's never happened to me, yes I have this boring habit of sticking to the rules, I hate you when you put on that air of moral superiority, oh well of course I realize the word 'moral' isn't one of your favourites. Anyway, after a few quite unpleasant days she decided that she had no desire to tear everything apart for a casual affair. Fun while it lasted, maybe, but only a casual affair. She promised she would break off the relationship, he believed her and for a while – maybe almost two years – they both pretended that everything was fine. Obviously it wasn't. Everything was wrong. So one day, as was only inevitable, she met someone else and went for it.

"I know I'm starting to sound like a slut, no, no, I'm sorry, don't interrupt, I know it isn't true and at the same time it is true. Of course I felt the need, or the desire, or whatever you want to call it, but at the same time I wanted to do something that would break everything up. I felt trapped and I was looking for a way to get out of the trap or, better still, smash it to pieces."

The previous pattern had repeated itself almost exactly, except that this time there was no screaming and shouting, no quarrels, no dithering. He had simply walked out. For days and days he hadn't answered the phone, hadn't called, hadn't let her know where he was, hadn't talked to their son.

As Emma continued with her story, her voice had become ever more neutral, ever more colourless, ever more monotone. There were no highs or lows. It seemed like the murky water of certain canals, the kind you have to look at carefully to see if it's moving or as still and dead as it seems.

141

"Exactly two weeks later, without our having spoken again, without his having even spoken to the child, he was in a road accident. He was on his moped and was knocked down and died on the spot, without suffering. Or at least that's what the doctors told me. Can you give me another cigarette?"

She smoked it entirely before telling him how everything had fallen to pieces. You want to say that it was all over anyway, you want to say that there's no connection between what you did and what happened. You want to say – you try to tell yourself – that it was a terrible tragedy that could have happened at any time. The voice that says all these things is drowned out by another much louder, much stronger voice, altogether capable of insinuating itself into the deepest fibres of your soul. This voice says something simple and deadly: it's your fault.

It's your fault.

It's your fault.

It's your fault.

Your mind starts to set in motion thoughts you weren't expecting. That you loved the man. That he was the only man you had ever really loved and you'll never love anyone again.

That if he hadn't left home, nothing would have happened to him.

That you killed him.

That you deprived your son of his father.

These last words struck Roberto full in the face, like a slap.

"Please don't."

"I'm sorry," she said, as if awakening from a bout of delirium. "I'm sorry," she said again after lighting another cigarette and immediately putting it out again without smoking it.

"I won't go into detail about the following months. I have the impression you don't need it. It was my mother who took me to our doctor. He's a friend of hers and she says he's one of the few around who's really good. I remember her words when she first went there with me, before she left me outside the front door."

"What did she say?"

"It was a very unusual phrase for my mother, who isn't a very expansive woman, but a practical woman even in the way she expresses herself. She said, 'He'll help you to go through the fire and survive.'"

Why was she telling him these things? And was she really telling him, or was it only an opportunity to get them off her chest, and whoever had been there would have done just as well? He looked at her, searching for an answer, but Emma's face was completely inscrutable. For a few seconds, her words lost their meaning and became only sounds, a rustle in the night and a face moving in the half-light.

When Roberto again heard her clearly, she was talking about her son.

"Giacomo writes very well, he writes things you'd think were by an adult – he takes after his father for that." She broke off, as if struck by a sudden intuition or a troublesome thought. "You see, I can't say his name, unless I deliberately force myself. *His father.*"

"What was his name?" Roberto asked, and as he did so it seemed to him that the question had a deeper meaning, a perfect rhythm that brought him back to what was happening tonight. She took a deep breath before she replied.

"Gianluca. His name was Gianluca. I've never liked composite names," she added, as if it were of crucial importance. Maybe it was.

"He was writing a novel. He was working as a screenwriter but his great dream was to write a novel. It's all in his computer, I think. I tried switching it on and it asked me for a password. It was a relief. I wanted to read what he'd written, but I was terribly afraid. I was afraid for various reasons. Obviously I was afraid to find things I wouldn't have liked to discover about him and about me. But you know, I was especially afraid of discovering that the novel wasn't any good. Anyway, luckily, the existence of the password solved the problem. It's impossible to gain access to that novel – that fragment of a novel or whatever it is – and that's it."

No, Roberto thought, that wasn't it. Getting into a computer protected by a common password was very easy. But that wasn't what Emma would have liked to hear him say, and he knew it. So they sat there in silence on the bench, while the background noises of the night took the place of their conversation.

After a while she seemed to be about to make a gesture. To move closer, to stretch out her hand. As if a command had come from her brain and had reached the edge of her body and there had been intercepted by another impulse, which had wiped everything out.

"I just remembered 'Stairway to Heaven'. It was his favourite song. The times in the past I've had to get it out of my head before I start crying. At the beginning the tears were faster than I was. Then I got good at it and managed to stop the song before I felt any emotion. Now it started again and I didn't notice. I heard it and it took me a while to realize what it was. And it didn't make me cry. It's made me a bit sad, but nothing like the desperation I used to feel."

She looked at her watch.

"Maybe it's time to go. I'm working tomorrow, although I don't start too early, not until ten. Something I miss from the days when I was an actress, and Giacomo wasn't even born yet, is being able to wake up late, to sleep all through the morning."

"Let's go to your garage, drop the bike and then I'll walk you home," Roberto said.

"No, I like the idea of taking you home."

Roberto liked the idea too.

As they were riding back through the deserted city, Roberto thought of their two lives as two trajectories that had begun more or less from the same point, had gone through different worlds and now had mysteriously crossed again.

"I wonder what your apartment is like."

"Unpresentable."

"Doesn't anyone ever come to see you?"

"A friend drops by sometimes, or a colleague. But that doesn't happen often."

"No girlfriends, nothing like that?"

Roberto shook his head and smiled, as if surprised by the question, as if it were a bit crazy, whereas in fact it was perfectly normal. You're a single man in good health. It would be only natural for you to see women. And yet the question strikes you as strange, misplaced.

"No, no girlfriends, nothing like that."

"All right, the tone of your answer and your expression tells me I shouldn't insist. Good night, then."

"Good night and thank you," Roberto said, awkwardly, but she did not go.

"Why did I tell you all those things?"

"Maybe it's passing."

"Maybe it's passing. You're right. Maybe I went through the fire and survived."

Roberto looked at her in silence.

"Aren't you going to say anything?"

"Maybe you went through the fire and survived," he said at last. "That's it. Maybe we survive."

145

19

She slipped into the room between the half-open door and the doorpost. She seemed thinner than last time, but maybe it was only an effect of the dim light. A window must have been open, because Roberto felt quite a strong shiver when she sat down on the bed. Of course, it was an unexpected visit, and at the moment it wasn't clear how she had come in. She had never had the key to this apartment. In fact, come to think of it, she had never been in this apartment, so how had she got in? Maybe he should just ask her. Except that speaking seemed terribly tiresome. Maybe the tiredness was all down to the fact that he'd been about to go to sleep.

She didn't seem to have any intention of breaking the silence. She sat there and waited. She must have got a lot thinner, Roberto thought. She hardly weighed anything at all. When she had sat down on the bed he had not felt her weight on the mattress. Again a cold draught. He had no idea which window was open. Maybe she had been the one to leave it open, whichever window it was. Maybe that was how she had got in. He should have got up and gone and closed it, but he was so tired, so terribly tired.

He couldn't even lift his arm. He couldn't move a single muscle; it was as if his whole body were paralysed.

Then she spoke, or rather, he heard her voice. The semi-darkness prevented him from seeing her lips moving, and the voice came from an unspecified point in the room. It was a bit different from the last time.

It was *different* from the last time.

You aren't asking me any questions.

That's because I can't find the words.

You haven't spoken Spanish for a long time.

Am I speaking Spanish? I hadn't realized.

You hadn't realized.

But is it a boy or a girl?

It's a boy.

What have you called him?

My father's name. What else?

But what does he know about *his* father?

He knows he's dead.

But I'm not dead.

She laughed, and the sound was like some mechanical device. Roberto thought he could smell a slight odour of rotten eggs.

You are dead, of course you're dead.

I had no choice.

I know, nobody has a choice.

How is he? How are your lives? Tell me.

They don't exist. Our lives.

What do you mean?

Nothing exists. For you we're a dream.

I didn't want it.

Nobody wants anything.

I'm scared.

You're right, it's scary.

I'd like to see the boy.

He's there.

Where?

Where you can't see him.

Why?

You'll never see him.

Why?

Because I don't exist, and neither do you.

Roberto sat up in bed, with difficulty, and reached out his hand to touch her or shake her or something else, he didn't know what. The hand passed through her and she slowly lowered her eyes, looking at his hand going through her. Roberto saw her tilted head, her hair, and at the same time, in an unnatural synchrony, he saw her face, her smiling mouth, which then burst wide open in a laugh and became the most frightening thing of all.

Just as Roberto was thinking that he would go mad with fear, everything suddenly disappeared and the room went back to normal.

Normal.

Giacomo

Ginevra came back to school today, but that's not good news.

She came in late, after the first hour had already started. As soon as I saw her I realized something was wrong. She was sloppily dressed, which has never happened before, not in all the time I've known her. But what struck me most of all was her expression. I watched her all through the five hours of lessons. She was absent, her eyes were staring, she didn't hear whenever anyone – not me, I didn't have the courage – said something to her, and she didn't smile once all morning.

The Italian teacher caught her not paying attention three times during her explanation and in the end gave her a warning. It was the first time I'd seen her get a warning in these last two years.

At the end of the fifth hour she left without talking to anybody, moving like a junkie, and didn't even seem to know where the way out was. There wasn't anyone waiting for her outside on a moped or anything like that. She left alone, after passing like a sleepwalker between all the boys and girls chatting and making a noise outside the main entrance.

I had a bad feeling as I went home, wondering what could have happened to her. I'd have liked to meet Scott immediately, to see what he thought and get his advice about what to do. It was such a strong need that after a while I even thought of trying to fall asleep just so that I could dream about him and talk to him.

I lay down on the bed, closed my eyes and tried to sleep, concentrating on the images of the park, and on Scott's face.

But it didn't work: I couldn't sleep, and when I got up after a while I felt very sad and alone.

20

"They're called hypnagogic illusions."

"What kind of illusions?"

"Hypnagogic illusions. They're a kind of hallucination. They occur in the transition phase between waking and sleep, which is actually called the hypnagogic phase. In that phase – which can last anything from a few seconds to several minutes – it's very difficult for the individual to distinguish dreams from reality. That's what happened to you. Did you also have the impression you couldn't move, that you were alert but paralysed?"

"Yes, that's it exactly. I was awake, my eyes were open and I was moving them, looking around, and I could speak – actually I think I did speak, I had a conversation with this person, I mean with this apparition – but I couldn't move. Yes, paralysed is the exact word."

"That's another characteristic of hypnagogic experiences – paralysis. On the whole it can be quite a troubling experience."

The doctor paused for rather a long time and looked Roberto in the eyes.

"In some cases it can even be a frightening experience."

And after another few minutes' silence: "Who was the person you saw?"

It was obvious he was going to ask that question. Roberto shouldn't have told him what had happened if he didn't want to hear that question. That much was clear.

Roberto took a pen from the desk, removed the cap, looked at the tip as if it were really interesting, then put the cap back and a few seconds later repeated the same sequence. And then again. And then yet again. The doctor watched him but did not intervene.

"Why don't you say anything?" Roberto asked, abruptly interrupting the obsessive rhythm of that movement.

"I'm afraid you're the one who should be saying something, if you want to."

Roberto resumed playing with the pen. A few minutes passed.

"You haven't answered my question."

"Maybe because I don't feel like it. Maybe because I don't want to talk about it."

"Talk about what?"

"As I said, I don't want to."

"Actually I think you do, but you can't summon up the courage. But maybe now's the time."

He was right, as always, and Roberto knew it. He felt his anger grow and break the bounds.

"What the hell are you talking about?"

"You tell me what we're talking about."

The doctor's voice was still calm, but there was a touch of hardness in it that Roberto couldn't stand. He felt as if he were about to lose control. He stood up and swept everything off the desk and onto the floor. The doctor made no attempt to stop him, did not even move his chair back, and said nothing.

"You know what I really don't want to do? I don't want to keep listening to your bullshit, so I'm going. I don't think I'll be back."

He felt the impulse to kick the desk, but managed to restrain himself. He left without turning round, but still seemed to see the doctor sitting motionless on his chair, watching him go out and disappear.

* * *

The days had got longer, Roberto thought as he came out of the building. It was still light and yet he was sure it had been dark at the same hour the previous time. Even though now he had come out at least half an hour early. Then he told himself that was absurd, that the previous time it must have been light as well, given that it was late April. Why, then, did he remember it as being dark, with the street all lit up as if it were winter? He would think it over later; right now he was confused. Very, very confused. And he felt a strong tingling sensation that started in the spine and went all the way to the groin.

"My nerves are on edge," he said aloud.

The tingling sensation became almost unbearable as Roberto walked, thinking all the while that he had no desire to walk.

There was a taxi at a stand he had never noticed before, a few hundred yards from the office. The driver was reading a magazine. Without thinking, Roberto got in. The driver put his magazine down on the seat next to him and turned round to greet his customer. He moved slowly and calmly. He was an elderly man. He even seemed too elderly to still be working. Judging by his appearance, he must have been about seventy, or just under. Roberto wondered if a man could still be driving a taxi at that age.

"Good evening, signore, where can I take you?"

Yes, where?

"I want you to show me Rome."

The driver looked at him with vague surprise. Show him Rome, in what sense? He smiled, waiting politely.

"Let's go to the Coliseum and to the Forum, to start with."

"Is this your first visit to Rome, signore?"

"Yes."

"I'll take you, signore, but it's late. By the time we get there they'll be closing and they won't let you in."

"Never mind. We'll stop and take a look out of the window. Then maybe I'll go back another time."

The man looked at him for a few seconds, then gave a slight shrug of his shoulders, turned, started the engine, and set off.

The movement of the car, the fact that there was a temporary destination to reach, calmed Roberto a little.

He had once read an article in an in-flight magazine about places of transit. The author of the article had talked about the comforting sense of temporariness we feel in places we arrive and leave from. Airports in particular, but also railway stations, bus stations, motels where you stop for just one night, where there's nothing around but a supermarket, a fast-food restaurant and a few houses where you can't imagine people actually living. The article spoke of our restlessness, our premature nostalgia for places we have to leave very quickly.

When he was working undercover, Roberto was always temporary, wherever he went. That was why he felt at ease in those situations, why he almost grew fond of the absurd routines of that fictitious existence. His condition was one of impermanence, and this, paradoxically, made him feel as if he wasn't temporary.

When everything had fallen to pieces, even that dubious equilibrium had been knocked for six. The prospect of staying in the same place, with the same identity, doing a normal job, had made him see, with sudden clarity, the absence of reference points in his life.

Now he was sitting in a taxi, without any reason or objective, without even a centre of gravity, riding along the streets of a city where he had lived for years and which he had never really got to know. He felt a sudden sensation of peace.

They turned into the Via dei Fori Imperiali and there ahead of them was the Coliseum.

"Do you want me to stop here, signore?"

He said yes, but in such a low voice that he had to repeat it to be heard.

The driver pulled up and Roberto got out. He only lived a few hundred yards away, and yet everything around him was completely unknown to him.

He felt as though he were hanging upside down in the air. And from that position he had the impression that he was starting to understand. He didn't know exactly what, but it seemed to him he was starting to understand.

Upside down like that, he felt that he was *seeing* what was around him. The world was acquiring a distinctness, a transparency, an intelligibility that hadn't existed before. The succession of arches and vaults enclosing windows of dark blue sky concealed a solution. The sky was taking on the form given to it by the Coliseum. In reality, Roberto was not seeing the Coliseum, he was seeing the sky as enclosed by the Coliseum. That altered perception gave him a sense that time was completely standing still.

"Excuse me, signore…"

"Yes?"

"We can't stay here too long. If the traffic police come by, they'll make me wish I'd never been born – or become a cab driver."

Roberto felt a surge of sympathy for the old man. He got back in the taxi and they drove off again, proceeding towards the Coliseum and then circling it.

"Is this really your first visit to Rome, signore?"

Roberto nodded, almost believing it himself.

The old man peered at him in the rear-view mirror.

"You are Italian, aren't you?"

He nodded again.

"How much time do you have?"

How much time did he have? In general, how much time

155

did he have? He heard himself say, "A couple of hours. Then I have an appointment."

"Do you like films, signore?"

Does anybody ever answer no to a question like that? Does anybody ever say they don't like films? Yes, he liked films, why did he ask?

"Seeing as how you want to do a quick tour of Rome, let me suggest something."

"What?"

"To see the city in a slightly different way."

"What kind of way?"

"Let's do a tour of the places where they shot the most famous films set in Rome. They're some of the most beautiful places in the city and so at least we have a theme for the ride. We have a – what can I say? – a yardstick. We have a yardstick. What do you think?"

We have a yardstick. It's a good thing to have a yardstick. Film locations as a yardstick. It had to mean something.

"Why not?"

The driver smiled, straightened a little on the seat, and when he started speaking again his tone was slightly different.

"Then let's start with *Roman Holiday*. Remember Gregory Peck and Audrey Hepburn riding round on a Vespa? One of the images on the posters was taken right here, as they were driving down the Via dei Fori Imperiali. Even though there was a bit less traffic in those days, shall we say."

Roman Holiday. Audrey Hepburn. A yardstick. They all say I look like Audrey Hepburn. Do these things happen by chance?

Roberto had fallen silent and the taxi driver peered into the rear-view mirror.

"You have seen the film, haven't you?"

"I've seen a few scenes, the odd clip. I've never seen the whole film."

156

"That's not good, signore. My father was an extra on that film, and I actually visited the set, though I don't remember much about it because I was small. At home I have a photo of my dad with Audrey Hepburn. God, she was beautiful. You remember her, don't you?"

Actually he didn't remember her very well because Emma's face was superimposed on hers. She resembled Audrey Hepburn, she had said. Roberto imagined the few scenes he knew of the film with an actress who was Emma, and he remembered that evening a few days earlier as if he had spent it with Audrey Hepburn, even though her face was very out of focus, almost unrecognizable.

All he said to the taxi driver was: yes, of course, he remembered her well. Which in a sense was true. As often happens, it was only part of the truth.

"You know what Gregory Peck did when they were shooting the film?"

"What did he do?"

"He was already a big star, whereas Audrey Hepburn was an almost unknown young actress. Gregory Peck's name should have been bigger in the credits, that was normal. After seeing how Audrey Hepburn acted, he asked for their two names to be the same size. He said Audrey Hepburn would win an Oscar and he didn't want to look like a fool, with his name bigger than the name of the Oscar winner in the credits of the film."

"And did she win an Oscar?"

"Of course. She won an Oscar and then lots of other awards. And Gregory Peck always said those months he spent in Rome were the happiest of his entire career."

Roberto did not say anything, but the driver did not notice. He seemed to have jumped at the opportunity of talking about his passion for films, and nothing was going to stop him.

157

"Of course, things were different in those days. The war was only just over. There was a hunger for life, a joy, a beauty, which are gone now. We're all sad now. Even though we may have more things. I'm also sadder now. But when I'm sad I know what to do. I watch one of those great films again and I feel like a different person. Anyway, we're just passing the Campidoglio on your right. They shot a scene from *Souvenir d'Italie* there, when cars could still get up there. Now look behind you, you can see the Vittorio Emanuele monument, right? Do you see the optical illusion, the way it looks like it's getting bigger? Like the beginning of *Cinema Paradiso*, which won the Oscar – you know it, surely? Now we're in the Piazza del Popolo, where they shot the famous encounter between Vittorio Gassman and Nino Manfredi in *We All Loved Each Other So Much*. I can't get to the Trevi Fountain with the taxi but a lot of things were shot there. The scene of Anita Ekberg bathing in the fountain, of course, but also the one where Audrey Hepburn gets her hair cut by a hairdresser on the square and the one where Totò sells the fountain to an American tourist. The Spanish Steps, where Satta Flores imitates the scene from *Battleship Potemkin*…"

It lasted an hour and a half, maybe, and at the end – after a quick trip to the Coppedè district where Dario Argento had shot *The Bird with the Crystal Plumage* – the old taxi driver dropped Roberto a few hundred yards from where he had picked him up.

"Thank you, signore," he said as he took the money. "I wish I had a customer like you every day."

21

He got out of the taxi and looked up at the windows. There was a gleam of pale blue light behind the window of the doctor's office. The light on the desk must still be on.

It was at this point that he wondered what to do. What to say to the doctor when he rang the bell? Paradoxically, it wasn't what he had done, the way in which he had left the office some hours earlier, that worried him the most. It was the fact that he didn't have an appointment. Because without an appointment, it was difficult, if not impossible, to talk to the doctor. This was the rule, never explicitly formulated, but always respected.

He could wait for him down here. And then? I'm really sorry, I got carried away. OK, thanks for the apology, see you in my office next Monday, now if you don't mind I'm going home. Or else, thank you, but it may be best if you find another shrink, please see my secretary as soon as possible and pay for the last few sessions.

At that moment the door opened and a somewhat overweight woman who might have been Indian or Bangladeshi appeared, dragging four or five rubbish bags behind her and with a holdall over her shoulder. Roberto held the door open, the woman smiled at him, thanked him and slipped away with unexpected agility.

As if he were about to do something forbidden, Roberto

watched the woman for a few seconds and once he was sure she wouldn't turn round, he entered the building. He climbed the stairs, reached the landing and rang the bell, without giving himself time to think.

The doctor opened the door after about thirty seconds, nodded in greeting, and then told him to come in. Roberto remained in the doorway.

"I'm sorry about… earlier."

"Come in," the doctor said again.

They entered the office. The desk was tidy again. Apart from everything else, a glass of amber liquid stood on it. From the cabinet behind him, the doctor took another glass and a bottle without a label.

"Would you like some? It's a home-made brandy, distilled by a friend of mine."

Roberto was about to say no thanks, but instead said yes. The doctor poured a little brandy in Roberto's glass, added a little to his own as if to make the levels equal, and sat down.

"For this evening, though, let's skip the medication."

"If you give me permission, I'll skip it for ever."

"I don't think there's long to go now." He took a sip and Roberto did the same. The taste of the brandy reminded him of military cordial, which he had last drunk maybe twenty-five years earlier.

"When you left, I got a phone call from the person who has the appointment after you, the last one of the afternoon. He couldn't come and so, all at once, my work day was over. We often underestimate the tranquillizing power of routine. Suddenly finding myself with nothing to do, after you'd left in that way…"

"I'm sorry, I —"

"Please don't apologize. As I was saying: I was left alone, without anything to do for the rest of the afternoon, so I felt the need to call my son. But as usual I couldn't get through to him. He won't call me back."

"I didn't know you had a son."

"He's thirty years old. Actually, nearly thirty-one – it's his birthday in a few days. He was born when I was twenty-six and maybe I was too young, I wasn't ready yet. Assuming there's a time when we are ready. He dropped out of university and I've always thought he did it to spite me. To shatter the expectations I had of him. Of course, that's an interpretation completely based on my own narcissism. Maybe the simplest explanation is that he didn't like studying, or didn't like the studies I'd chosen for him. Anyway, now he works as a clerk in a finance company. It isn't exactly what I'd imagined for him. But to tell the truth, I didn't devote much time to imagining anything for him, and maybe that's the problem. We never see each other and I don't know anything about him, what he thinks, what he likes, what he hates – apart from me – his political ideas, if he has any. I don't know if he reads books – I suspect not – if he goes to the cinema, if he listens to music. I don't even know if he has a girlfriend. We only speak if I phone him, he never phones me. And when I phone him he's put out. I ask him how he is and he tells me he's fine as usual, and in an effort at politeness asks me if I'm fine, too, and I tell him yes, I'm fine, too, and I sense his impatience, I sense that he can't wait to hang up, whereas what I want is to ask him if he'd like to meet me, to talk properly, but I can never summon up the courage and our telephone calls always end up being sad and dreary."

He took a sip of brandy, then another, and then emptied the glass.

"Obviously we shouldn't be having this conversation. When you rang the bell I shouldn't have opened, or, alternatively, I should have told you I'd see you at our next appointment.

161

Anything except invite you in to have a drink with me and put up with the confessions of a failed father."

They were silent for a long time.

"I often think about my son too," Roberto said at last.

The doctor looked at him.

22

"I can't remember if I ever told you what my code name was."

"No, what was it?"

"Mongoose."

"That's the animal, a bit like a marten, that can kill a cobra, isn't it?"

"Yes, we almost all had animal names. Do you know why the mongoose can kill a cobra and snakes in general?"

"I suppose because it's very fast and can grab the snake by the throat before the snake has a chance to bite it."

"That's true, but sometimes the cobra manages to inject its poison all the same, and still nothing happens to the mongoose."

"Do you mean they have a kind of immunity to snake poison?"

"Yes. They have a defence mechanism – it has something to do with chemical receptors – identical to that of snakes. Which is why snakes aren't poisoned and killed by the toxins they themselves produce."

"Who gave you that code name?"

"One of our captains. But he didn't know that bit about poison and immunity. Neither did I. It's something I only discovered years later, reading an article. At the time I just registered the information. Then I remembered it, a little while later, and it seemed to me that it had a meaning. The mongoose, even if you hunt it down, is like a snake: it can live with poison in its body."

The doctor seemed to be about to say something. Then he had second thoughts.

"For many years I lived with criminals. They trusted me – in fact, they admired me – and I was working to bring them down, even when, as sometimes happened, we'd become friends. And you know why I was so good at that job?"

"Why?"

"Because I was like them. For example, I liked stealing. When you're working undercover you have money and means at your disposal that a normal carabiniere couldn't even dream about. You have lots of ways to pocket quite a bit of money or use it for different purposes that have nothing to do with your mission. That's what I did. I didn't feel any sense of guilt. In fact, I liked it. I liked it a lot."

Roberto emptied his glass and asked if he could have some more.

The doctor opened a drawer, took out a packet of chocolate biscuits and pushed it into the middle of the desk, halfway between them.

"Maybe we should eat something too."

They ate the chocolate biscuits and drank some more brandy, without speaking for a couple of minutes.

"My job was to be someone else. And it's not at all bad to be someone else from time to time: it makes you feel free. The problem arises when you have to be someone else most of the time. The problem arises when you have to be someone else in order to feel yourself. And when you're not someone else you know you're out of place. I don't know how to explain it."

"You couldn't have explained it any better."

"And anyway, I liked the company of criminals. Obviously to do my job properly, I had to act in such a way that they trusted me, but I know I did more than that. I wanted their approval, I wanted them to *like* me."

"Can you give me an example?"

"When I heard that one of the bosses had said I was a good boy, or a reliable guy, or that I really knew what I was doing, I was happy. Much happier than when my colleagues or my superior officers said similar things. I wanted to nail them, yes, but before anything else I wanted to win them over."

"How long did this last?"

Roberto tried to smile, but what emerged was a grimace.

"Do you mind if I light a cigar?" the doctor asked.

"No, not at all. And can I smoke a cigarette?"

"But let's not tell my other patients about this irregular session, all right?"

Roberto had the distinct sensation, or rather the certainty, that the doctor knew about him and Emma. It was a reassuring sensation, like a signal that things were going in the right direction.

From a drawer of the desk – the same one where the biscuits had been – the doctor took a box of Tuscan cigars. He took one out, cut it in the middle with a penknife, poured a little more brandy in the glasses and lit the cigar. Roberto lit his cigarette.

"There's a point I'd like to clarify before you continue with your story."

"Yes?"

"If you had the opportunity now, would you still like to steal? If you had the opportunity – in the same conditions, with a guarantee of impunity – would you like to go back to breaking the rules?"

Roberto stiffened on his chair, surprised. That wasn't the question he been expecting and he had no answer ready. It took him a few minutes to formulate one.

"I don't think so. I can't be sure, but I don't think so."

"When did you realize – when did you start to realize – that you didn't like it any more?"

Roberto lit another cigarette with the stub of the first. An action he hadn't performed for quite some time.

"I couldn't say for sure, but there are a few episodes, all from the last years, that always come into my mind together, one after the other."

"Then maybe you *can* say for sure."

"Maybe I can, now that you've made me think about it." And then, after a long pause, spent putting his thoughts and memories in order: "Yes, that's how it is. There were these three episodes when I should have realized that the machine wasn't working any more, the mechanism was breaking down, and it was probably time to stop."

"Then tell me about them. And if it's all the same to you, tell me about them in chronological order, from the oldest to the most recent."

*　*　*

It was in Mexico, in a small town close to the border with Arizona, and he was working in partnership with an officer from the federal police, who was also undercover.

There had been a working dinner at the house of a local chief; they had eaten and drunk and finalized their business. Now they were smoking and drinking and telling each other stories, more or less true, more or less invented.

The host was a man named Miguel, known as El Pelo. He had had a hair transplant, and dyed not only the hair on his head but also his pubic hair. He boasted of only having sex with girls less than twenty, which he said helped to keep him young.

After a while, El Pelo made a sign to one of his two body-guards. The man went out and soon afterwards came back accompanied by three young girls. In actual fact, they were not much more than children, one of them especially. They were heavily made-up and dressed like whores, but under the make-up and the clothes it was perfectly obvious they were no more than twelve, the youngest probably even younger. There was an excited buzz in the big dining room.

El Pelo was smiling smugly. He was proud of his hospitality: a perfect host who knows what a real party is and doesn't simply offer wine and food and liqueurs. With a regal gesture, he announced that, in honour of his guests, he had bought three virgins, never touched by anyone before tonight. His favourite kind of merchandise. He concluded his brief speech by telling his guests to help themselves – *que aprovechen.*

The Mexican federal officer realized that something might be about to happen that couldn't be undone: Roberto could well say or do something that would blow the whole thing sky high. He hissed in his ear not to do anything stupid. There was nothing they could do about any of this, he said, nothing at all. The only thing that would happen is that their cover would be blown and they'd be killed. Roberto seemed not to hear. His colleague had to squeeze his arm until the nails penetrated the skin.

"Roberto, don't do anything stupid," he repeated. "Just think, soon we'll have all these sons of bitches arrested. And they'll pay for this too."

The scene in front of them was frighteningly grotesque. Hairy bellies, sweaty, contorted faces, animal-like sneers. Some of the men pressed round the girls' bodies, while others watched and masturbated.

Roberto and the Mexican officer waited until several men had drifted away and so there was no risk of being conspicuous, then went out onto the patio, lit cigarettes and smoked in silence.

* * *

Roberto passed a hand furiously over his face, almost as if trying to remove something sticky and tenacious. The doctor's face was motionless, his complexion had turned livid, and his tight lips formed a scar.

"I watched the rape of three little girls and I couldn't do anything. And you know what the worst part of it was?"

"What?"

"The girls were – how can I put this? – consenting. It wasn't rape in the sense of physical violence. They… *went along with it*, and the frightening thing was their smiles and their eyes. I tried not to watch but always ended up meeting the eyes of the youngest one. No. Meeting isn't the right word. She wasn't looking at anything, her eyes were open but they were like those of a dead girl."

He couldn't go on. He remembered the murder victims he had seen in his life. Murder victims always have their eyes open. Open in terror or surprise or both at the same time. We close the eyes of the dead because we can't bear to look at them, open onto nothing, lifeless. The memory of that evening in Mexico was silent. He couldn't remember the voices, or the cries, or the laughter, or the grunts. Only an unbearable mechanism of bodies and a line of distorted faces, a silent inferno.

The doctor's voice interrupted the nightmare.

"Tell me the second episode."

Roberto moved his head, like someone abruptly waking up and needing a few seconds to return to reality.

"I was in Madrid, handling a major deal involving Colombians, Spaniards and Italians. The Italians weren't the usual traffickers, Mafia, Camorra. They were – how can I put this? – normal guys who'd managed to get into the big time, which was quite unusual. You may have heard of the operation, I mean when we arrested them, because that unusual aspect of it caused a bit of a stir. Anyway, I was in Madrid with one of these guys, we had half a day free and he asked me if I wanted to go with him to visit a museum where there's this big, very famous painting by Picasso. The painting is called *Guernica* – I'm sure you know it – but I can't remember the name of the museum."

"The Reina Sofía."

"That's it, the Reina Sofía. Roberto – he had the same name as me – had already been to see *Guernica* several times and whenever he was in Madrid he always went back. He was a nice guy, with lots of interests. He was like, I don't know, a university teacher, a good schoolmate. The kind who finishes the work before the others and then passes the copy around. I liked talking to him and I think he liked talking to me. He said he thought I was different from the other people we had to deal with in our work. He meant our work as traffickers. He said he trusted me."

"Why was he a trafficker?"

"I don't know. He came from a good family, he'd been to university, he only had a few more exams to take and he could have graduated. I often thought of asking him why he was involved in trafficking, but I never did."

"Were you afraid of making him suspicious?"

"Yes, it's not the kind of question you ask in those circles. And anyway, if I'd asked him I think I know what he would have replied."

"What?"

"He would have said there was nothing bad about dealing in cocaine, nothing immoral. He would have said there's no real difference between drugs, cigarettes and alcohol. Except that the first are forbidden and the others aren't. If someone said something like that to me today I think I'd agree with him."

"Did you go to the Reina Sofía?"

"Yes, we went, and he told me a whole lot of things about *Guernica*. I remember hardly anything, apart from the thing about the Minotaur being a symbol of evil and bestiality."

Roberto broke off. A shudder went through him, as if due to a sudden fever, and he pursed his lips.

"A few months later I had him arrested along with lots of others. He was given fourteen years. I think he's still inside. All thanks to me, his friend. The man he trusted."

* * *

The third episode had taken place in Panama.

Roberto was a guest at the farm of a man connected to the Cali cartel in Colombia. The man was a very important person and the farm was a crazy place: there were tennis courts, an indoor Olympic-size swimming pool, another huge pool outside with artificial waves, and a regulation-size football pitch with grass that was watered every day and actual terraces. There was even a fake volcano that produced eruptions to order.

Real professional teams played on the football pitch, invited and paid for by the host. The matches were organized to entertain the guests. And all the rest was there to astonish visitors, who included police officers, mayors, politicians and professionals, as well as, of course, criminals and Mafiosi from all over.

While Roberto was there, a new shipment of arms arrived. Pump action rifles, assault rifles, guns of every kind. They just needed to be tried, and someone said it would be more fun to practise on living targets. The edge of the village a few miles from the farm was home to groups of semi-domesticated dogs, and this same person said that the dogs would make ideal targets. So they set off in a couple of jeeps loaded with people and arms and went in search of the dogs. In the end they found them, got out of the vehicles, and the weapons were loaded and handed out. Roberto got his gun too, and almost instinctively cocked the trigger.

A few people laughed, a few made jokes, a few said not to shout too loud because the dogs might escape. But the animals didn't even think of escaping. They were used to people and just stood there thirty or forty feet away, calm and trusting. Some lying asleep, others searching in the rubbish, the puppies playing.

Then the host raised his rifle – naturally it was up to him to start – unhurriedly took aim and fired. The first animal hit was a calm-looking ginger-coloured dog, some kind of Labrador. The shot hit it in the back part of its body, its legs gave way and it collapsed to the ground. Then all hell broke loose, a hell of fire and explosions and barking and whimpering and shouts and laughter and the smell of gunfire and smoke. Some dogs fell immediately, hit by the first volley. The others were pursued, and only a few managed to escape. Then the shooting stopped, and Roberto found himself standing there deafened in the middle of the smoke, with his pistol in his hand. Only then did he realize that he too had fired, like all the others.

Reloading the weapons, they advanced in scattered formation towards the place where most of the animals had fallen.

A guy nicknamed El Chico because of his baby face blew away the dying puppies with a round of M16 fire. Others took aim at the survivors as they tried to escape. Some attacked the animals that were already dead.

The dog that had been hit first, the one that looked like a Labrador, was still alive. It must have had its hip shattered, and was making high-pitched whines and flailing with its hind legs in a desperate attempt to get back on its feet.

Roberto approached it, cocked the trigger and shot it in the head. Blood and brain matter spattered on his trousers as the animal's body was shaken by a final shudder and fell still.

* * *

"I feel as ashamed as if it had happened yesterday. I couldn't prevent that massacre any more than I could prevent the rape of the three girls. But nobody forced me. I could have fired into the ground, or in the air, or not fired at all. I chose to take part."

"You shot the Labrador because you didn't want it to suffer."

"I'm a coward, a bastard, a piece of shit. The reason I was so good at working among criminals is because I'm like them. I belong with them, I —"

"That's enough now!" The doctor's voice was like a slap, rapid and well-aimed.

Roberto gave a start, just as if he had indeed been struck, and dropped his head. After a few seconds he raised it again and for no particular reason started inspecting the ceiling of the room. He looked at the highest shelves in the bookcases, then at a thin stucco frieze that ran parallel to the edge of the ceiling, some ten inches below it, then at a small crack in the plaster on which he focused for several seconds, as if the solution to everything were hidden just beneath it.

At last he turned his gaze towards the doctor. His eyes were moist and red. He sniffed, trying to do so in a polite way.

The doctor handed him a packet of paper handkerchiefs.

"But these weren't the things you *didn't* want to talk about this afternoon, were they?"

"No, they weren't," Roberto said, drying his eyes.

Giacomo

I woke up very early this morning, feeling very thirsty, and got up to go and drink a glass of water. I had already drunk all of the glass I had on the bedside table during the night without even waking up, as always happens to me. I drink in my sleep and in the morning I always find the glass empty and never remember drinking. When I was very small I was convinced it was a ghost that came and drank my water.

When I entered the kitchen I saw Mum there, sitting next to the open window. She had her back to me and didn't hear me come in. She was looking out of the window and crying.

It had been a long time since I had last seen her cry, and I froze. I would have liked to give her a hug and tell her there was no reason for her to be so sad, because I was there. But I couldn't do it – I *never* can. Instead, scared she would turn round, see me and lose her temper because I'd seen her cry, I crept silently away, went back in my room and sat down on the bed.

I was sure she hadn't heard or seen me. But after a few minutes she came into my room and also sat down on the bed, next to me. She had stopped crying, but was sniffing a bit. She had cleaned her teeth – I could smell the tooth-paste – but I still noticed that she had smoked a cigarette. Or maybe more than one. She took my hand and we sat like

173

that in the same position, hand in hand. The light from the corridor came in through the half-open door.

"Sometimes I'm a bit sad," she said without changing position. I nodded. I didn't know what to say, or maybe I knew what I should have said but didn't know how to say it. I wondered what our life would have been like if Dad hadn't died. It struck me that life is very unfair. I felt like crying and I made a great effort to stop myself.

"You know, when you grow up sometimes you're afraid of time passing. It's a difficult thing to explain, but the older you get the faster time seems to go. That's what makes you afraid."

She looked at me to see if I was following her. I nodded even though I wasn't terribly sure what she was saying.

"Sometimes, when I was young, I met friends of my grand-parents who maybe hadn't seen me for some years. People I didn't even remember. Everyone always said how incredible it was, I'd become a woman, how time flies. It seems like only yesterday you were just a little girl. It got on my nerves when they said that kind of thing. It seemed such crap…" She broke off. Mum is always very careful about swearing. She says it's not just a question of good upbringing and not being vulgar, and that the way in which we speak influences the way we think. I'm not sure of that, but I suspect this was something that Dad used to say.

"I'm sorry, Giacomo. It just came out. When you're tired or sad it happens. Anyway, I wanted to say this: when I heard those phrases, so many years ago, they seemed to me like nonsense. But now I understand."

It seemed to me she wanted to add something, but she didn't. Maybe she thought it was too complicated for someone my age. So she gave me a big hug, and I smelt her motherly smell, from when I was little, and we stayed like that, until the sadness went away a bit.

23

"I was working with an agent from the DEA, who was under-cover like me, and in association with the Spanish police and special departments of the Colombian police."

"The DEA is the American narcotics agency?"

"Yes. Often it's difficult to distinguish one of their under-cover agents from a real trafficker. But I think the same could have been said of me. His name was Phil, and right from the start I didn't like him at all. There was something... I can't find the word, maybe rotten, about him. He made such a negative impression on me that in the preparatory phrase of the operation I thought seriously of asking to be replaced."

Roberto stopped to think, wondering what would have happened if he had obeyed that impulse. He dismissed the thought immediately.

"Obviously I didn't. One of the aims of the investigation was to identify a network of members of the police and the drugs agencies – Italian, Spanish and American – who were in the pay of the traffickers. People who'd been untouchable up until then. And that was why, during the whole operation, relations with my covering team – the colleagues who were following my work and were supposed to intervene in case of emergency – were kept to a minimum. Every contact could be very dangerous."

"How long did the operation last?"

"More than a year and a half. I was in Colombia almost uninterruptedly for almost a year, by far the longest period I spent in South America. I had an apartment in Bogotá, I lived there, I was there for six months consecutively, without ever coming back. I know Bogotá much better than Rome, and I liked being there. I liked a lot of things about Bogotá."

"Such as?"

"First of all, the climate. It's close to the Equator but it's at an altitude of eight thousand five hundred feet. It's never really hot and never really cold. There's hardly any difference between the seasons, it's like spring all the year round. Then I liked the old city – La Candelaria – a place that's still dangerous but very beautiful. The taxi drivers always told you, almost obsessively, to keep your doors firmly locked, and sometimes, at night, you had the impression that small bands of ghosts had materialized in the streets, ready to strike and then disappear again."

"But you were armed?"

"No, though most of the people I was with were. And yet I never had any problems, even when I went around alone and unarmed. In Bogotá you find things you don't expect. For example, there's an incredible tram system – the TransMilenio, a kind of surface metro – that works like clockwork: you feel as if you're in Stockholm or Zurich. Then there are streets closed to traffic where you can't even park a car. You imagine a South American capital – and especially Bogotá, which has such a terrible reputation – as a place where cars are one on top of the other, double- and triple-parked, just like here in Rome. Well, I lived in an apartment on the fifteenth floor in a residential neighbourhood, and at night I'd open my window – the air was always cool and never cold – I'd light a cigarette, look out at the empty streets and feel a sense of peace. I liked it a lot."

"I wouldn't have thought so."

"It's a surprising place. They have a national library in La Candelaria which they say is the most visited library in the world."

Roberto broke off, rubbed his eyes with his fingertips and massaged his temples.

"You were telling me about the library."

"Yes. Actually I never went in, I only saw it from the outside. Somebody told me about it…"

All at once Roberto had the feeling he was talking in a language he barely knew. He couldn't find the words in Italian, although complete sentences came to him in English or Spanish. This lasted some twenty or thirty seconds, then things returned to their place.

"A girl. She was the one who told me about the library. She was almost twenty years younger than me and she was the daughter of one of the men we were investigating. I met her at her father's house and after two days it was as if we'd known each other for ever. Nothing like that had ever happened to me before."

"Was she beautiful?"

"She wasn't only beautiful. She was intelligent, she was deep, she was full of passion. And she was friendly, she made me laugh, she made me feel like a better man than I am. She was the most extraordinary person I've ever met."

"What did she do?"

"She was a student, she was about to graduate in literature, and she had no connection with what her father did. When she realized I was in business with him, which happened almost immediately, she started talking to me about the possibility of changing our lives. She said she'd like to leave there and come to Italy. We could open a shop, or a little hotel, anything to have a normal life."

"And what did you say?"

"I said it would be wonderful. And like a madman, I really thought things would somehow sort themselves out and we'd be able to do it."

"Can you tell me her name?"

Roberto stared at him in surprise. The doctor returned his gaze, expectantly.

"Now that you ask me, I realize I probably never called her by her name. We didn't call each other by our names. We said the kind of things to each other that lovers say, the kind you later feel ashamed to repeat. I called her darling and sweetheart, in Italian. She liked to hear me talk in Italian. It's taken me a few seconds to remember her name. It was Estela."

"Why the past tense?"

"I'm sorry?"

"Why do you say her name *was*?"

Instinctively, Roberto moved his head back and to the side, as if he were about to receive a slap or a punch and he wanted to soften the blow.

"I didn't realize. She isn't dead… I think. I don't know why I used the past tense."

"Is she the person in your dream?"

"Yes."

A long pause. Like a final summing-up, a silent, rapid, conclusive settling of accounts.

"I shouldn't have got involved, of course. But at first I told myself it was only a fling – I'd had others during my missions – even though everything told me this was something different. With any other woman it would never have happened. I've never loved a woman the way I loved her."

And then, after a few minutes' pause, after superimposed images that did not respect the rules of chronology: "Things were gradually wearing me down, and I couldn't control it. I continued doing my work – gathering information, sending reports, organizing shipments of cocaine and preparing the arrests – and at the same time I was living another life, in which I was a man in love, I did romantic things and indulged in absurd plans for the future. I was completely unaware of what I was doing, and I didn't realize I was heading towards a precipice."

"How long did it last?"

Once again, Roberto seemed surprised by the question. He had to think a lot before he found the answer. When he did, he seemed even more surprised.

"Six months, maybe a little more. If I hadn't thought specifically about the time I would have said it had lasted much longer."

"You have an inflated perception of that time."

"Yes, that's exactly it. As the moment approached when the final part of the operation would get under way and I'd have to disappear, I pretended that everything was fine, hoping there'd be some kind of magic solution that would solve everything, without anybody getting hurt."

"Was her father one of those you were hoping to arrest?"

"He was one of the most important. He wasn't just a trafficker, he was in charge of vast quantities of money and also controlled the political side of things. On the one hand, he could get members of parliament and mayors elected, and on the other he was in direct contact with violent criminals all over the world. There was even a group of Colombian police officers who when they'd finished their day's work – their regular work – did a few hours for him as bodyguards. It had been extremely difficult to get close to him, this was the most important operation of my life, and I'd got myself involved with his daughter. Every time the thought went through my head, my legs started to shake. I dismissed it, telling myself that when the right moment came I'd find a way to sort things out."

"And then the moment arrived."

"And then the moment arrived," Roberto repeated. "We'd organized a shipment by sea. A ship literally filled with cocaine. Tons of it. In the previous months, with my work, and Phil's, and intercepts in various countries – especially in Italy – we'd gathered enough evidence to put hundreds of people in prison. My task was over and I was supposed to go back to Italy. Obviously what all those people thought, starting with José – Estela's father – was that I was going to Italy to supervise the final stages of the shipment. Which was true, of course, but not in the way they understood. I'd told them that once the operation was over, I'd be back in Colombia within a few weeks. The real reason I had to go back to Italy was that when the shipment arrived at its destination, there'd be arrests and confiscations all round the world. The last place I ought to be, at that point, was Bogotá."

"Did this… José know about you and his daughter?"

"I think so, even though nothing was ever said openly. In any case we didn't hide it. I don't think José knew quite how to react to the matter. He liked me and trusted me. On the other hand he knew I was a drug trafficker like him and he wasn't happy that his daughter was with somebody who did the same work as him. Typical of criminals trying to turn themselves into legitimate businessmen. Anyway, he didn't do anything to stand in our way, she… we enjoyed complete freedom. It was the happiest and craziest time of my life."

Roberto took a series of deep breaths.

"It was just a few days before I was due to leave that Estela told me she was expecting a baby. She wanted to keep it. I was in a trance. I said yes, I wanted it too. She hugged me tight, and she was so happy – she was crazy with happiness because of the baby – that I felt my heart breaking. That's not just an image: as she held me tight I really felt a physical pain in the middle of my chest. So strong that I thought I was going to have a heart attack. That night I didn't sleep a wink. I seemed to be suffocated by anxiety, though actually *I seemed* isn't the right expression. I *was* suffocated by anxiety. And along with anxiety there was panic."

Roberto rocked back and forth on his chair, apparently unable to control himself. He picked up the packet of cigarettes, took one out and lighted it. The doctor asked for one for himself too.

"The days that passed between the news of the pregnancy and my departure were a nightmare. When my mother died a few years ago, I felt enormously sad. When my father was arrested and then died it was terrible. But there's nothing I can compare to what I experienced then. I couldn't eat, I couldn't sleep, I had to be careful not to start crying in public. Sometimes I caught myself repeating a gesture or a movement obsessively – I don't know, walking round and round an armchair or constantly shifting an object on a table – like animals at the zoo that go crazy in cages. And you know what the worst of all was?"

"What?"

"Talking to Phil, the DEA agent. He was pleased that everything was coming to an end and we could get out of there. I was desperate and had to pretend to be as pleased and relieved as he was. With Estela on the other hand, I had to pretend to be happy about the future that was waiting for us, the fact that we'd be getting married, and we were going to have a baby, and that we'd give it an Italian name because she liked Italian and we'd live in Italy, which was the most beautiful country in the world…"

The doctor put out his cigarette, crushing it in the ashtray with more force than necessary.

"Was there a moment when you thought of telling her how things were?"

"Yes. I thought of telling her the truth and asking her to run away with me, but it was a completely mad idea. How could she come with me when I was sending her father to prison, maybe for the rest of his life? Then I thought of blowing the operation, quitting the Carabinieri and everything else, and staying with Estela in Colombia. I thought about that seriously – or rather I like to *think* I thought about it seriously – but I didn't have enough courage to do something like that. So when the day came for me to leave, I went to say goodbye to José, hugged him and told him I'd see him in a month. Then I went to see Estela and as she kissed me she told me she'd miss me terribly, that she'd count the minutes until I got back, and that meeting me had been the most beautiful thing that had ever happened to her. I told her it had been the same for me, and I was telling the truth."

Roberto had spoken with his head down, his eyes fixed on the wooden surface of the desk. Having reached this point, he looked up and his eyes met the doctor's.

"I left and never saw her again."

It was like a sudden silence after a deafening noise.

Roberto took one hand in the other, swayed forward for a few seconds, and then remained motionless, staring into the air. The pain slowed. And of course, it was pain, but less unbearable than this thing that had remained closed up for so long. It lasted a while.

"*Over the Rainbow*. That was the code name."

"I'm sorry?"

"*Over the Rainbow* was the code name for the operation."

"Like the song."

"Like the song, yes."

The operation had reached its climax, with arrests all over the world, and confiscations of companies, money, drugs, cars. It was one of the most important operations in the history of the war on drugs.

Obviously, Estela's father was among those arrested.

Roberto's colleagues couldn't understand why he took no interest in the arrests and the start of legal proceedings. He seemed apathetic, even after three weeks' leave and the news that he had been put forward for a solemn commendation. He started working again but no longer seemed the same person, either to his colleagues or his superiors. His superiors realized almost immediately that now was not the time to give him any difficult new assignments. And after a few months everyone realized that now was not the time to give him any assignments at all. Sometimes people caught him talking to himself in the office. Others met him, still by himself, dressed in rumpled clothes – he had always been so careful about his appearance – his eyes red and watery with alcohol, his beard long, his back stooped, a cigarette always hanging from the corner of his mouth. And then that young officer found him in the office, with the barrel of his gun in his mouth and the empty expression of someone who was already on the other side.

They had asked him to hand over his gun and had given him leave for health reasons. A neutral expression meaning that he had gone mad, that he was unfit for duty, a danger to himself and others.

"Maybe ten months had passed when I found the courage to call a colleague in the Colombian national police. Someone I'd become almost friends with. I thought of beating about the bush and letting the question come out as if it was just idle curiosity. But then I realized I had no desire to play games. Let him think whatever he wanted. I asked him for information about Estela. I asked him if her father was still inside, if she'd been dragged into the investigation in any way, and if she was still living in Bogotá. I asked him to let me know everything he could."

"What did he say?"

"He didn't make any comment, didn't even ask me why I

183

wanted the information. All he said was that he'd need two or three days. He was as good as his word. On the third day he called me and told me what he'd managed to find out: Estela was still living in Bogotá, in her father's house, and had been left out of the investigation. She went regularly to see her father in prison. Before telling me the last piece of information, he hesitated for a few seconds, and at that moment I was absolutely certain he knew everything about me and her."

"What did he tell you?"

"Something he'd got from one of his informants. He told me that a couple of months after the arrests Estela had been admitted to a private clinic, where she'd had an abortion. In secret, because abortion is illegal in Colombia. The baby she aborted was my son."

There Roberto's story broke off, like a street that comes to a sudden dead end.

According to the wall clock, it was after two. The doctor stood up to open the window and let the smoke dissipate. The air was mild and there weren't many cars passing. The night air carried a vague, premature scent of lime trees.

"It's time for bed," the doctor said, going back towards the desk but without sitting down. Roberto stood up, and it seemed to him as if the muscles of his legs had lost all their elasticity.

"What… What happens now?"

The doctor smiled. His eyes were half closed and he looked tired.

"Have you ever told that story before?"

"Never, and I didn't even think I'd be capable of it."

"There you are: you didn't think you'd be capable and yet you were. The rest will come." After a moment he added, "Anyway, I'll see you on Monday, if you want. But if you feel you need a break, that's fine too. You don't have to tell me now."

When they reached the door, Roberto couldn't make up his mind to leave.

"You think about that child as if it had been born, don't you?"

"Yes. I think about it as if it had been born, as if it were a boy, and as if it had grown. I imagine him as a little boy…"

"It'll pass. It's going to take time and a bit of patience, but it'll pass."

Roberto nodded, and the doctor did the same.

"We've followed a somewhat unorthodox procedure. A midnight session with brandy and chocolate. Maybe I'll write a paper about it for the next conference. Maybe I've invented a new protocol."

Giacomo

I was in the park with Scott, but I don't know how and when I'd got there.

A few yards ahead, with her back to us, was Ginevra.

I called to her, but she didn't move.

I called again and she started walking, fast like in the other dream. I set off in pursuit of her again and this time I managed to keep behind her, even though I couldn't get any closer: however hard I tried, the distance between us always remained the same. Scott followed me without saying a word, but I could sense that he was worried.

After a while she came to a door that seemed to have materialized out of nowhere, right there in the middle of the grass, complete with frame and handle. To my enormous surprise Ginevra opened it, went in and disappeared, as if there was a house or a room or something behind the door.

But there was only lawn. I walked around it two or three times and that's all there was.

"What is this door, Scott?"

Forget about it, chief. Let's get out of here.

"What do you mean, let's get out of here? What happened to Ginevra?"

Scott sighed and sat down. He seemed worried.

Ginevra is in her room, asleep. Now let's get out of here.

"I'm going through, she needs my help."

I wouldn't do that, chief.

"I'm going."

I didn't wait for his reply and didn't even look at him. I opened, went in, closed the door behind me and found myself in a dark room. There was a slight scent in the air and it took me a while to realize that it was Ginevra's. When my eyes were accustomed to the darkness, I started to make out what was in the room. A desk with a computer, exercise books, pens, magazines; a cabinet with one door half open; shelves with dolls, a few books, a radio, a little TV set; a lopsided Justin Bieber poster – I think he's a real idiot, but the girls like him a lot.

And then the bed, where Ginevra was fast asleep, even though she'd only got in a few seconds earlier.

I went closer. Her breathing was a bit irregular, she had her arms round the pillow, and she looked very beautiful. After a while I saw her purse her lips, like someone who's about to start crying and is trying to restrain themselves.

"Help…" she whispered.

"What's the matter?" I asked, but she didn't hear me. She was asleep.

"Please help me…"

"I *want* to help you. But you must tell me what's going on."

She didn't hear me, and after a few seconds she started crying in her sleep.

The whole thing made me crazy. I had to wake her, I thought, and tell her not to cry, tell her I was there to protect her and she just had to tell me what was going on and I would solve everything. So I put a hand on her shoulder and at that precise moment I felt a kind of electric shock spreading from my hand all over my body. I had a frightening vision – dozens of devils jumping on me all together with a disgusting noise – and then I woke up with a start, as if someone had flung me from one side to the other.

* * *

187

I'd never before woken up like that since I'd been going to the park.

I woke up full of nasty premonitions, and it wasn't a good day, after that dream and that awakening. At school I was more distracted than usual and the maths teacher got quite angry. She said it was as if I wasn't in class but always somewhere else.

Ginevra too – as always since she'd come back – was completely distracted. It seemed to me that we were like two strangers in that class. For different reasons we were completely out of place.

When we left school I followed her. I saw her walking away quickly, almost as if escaping. So I ran along the other side of the street, went about fifty yards past her, then crossed over and turned back as if that was my direction.

I don't know what I wanted to do. Maybe I wanted to stop her and talk to her, ask her what was wrong, offer her my help.

But when we came level she didn't even look at me, didn't even *see* me. She passed right by me and was gone.

24

Roberto set off and the memories of childhood suddenly came crowding in. Some were set in the welcoming semi-darkness of his childhood home, others in the sunlight and the blinding foam of the waves.

The memories set in his home were full of little noises, a constant, benevolent murmur: the door of his bedroom opening and closing with a familiar, reassuring creak; his mother talking on the phone in English with the Italian accent she was so proud of; water running in the bathroom; the voices on television when he was already in bed at night; his mother's soft, slightly shuffling footsteps early in the morning.

The memories of light and sea, on the other hand, were silent. Cool wind, waves with glossy crests, surfboards running, bodies tossed by the power of the water. All without noise and without voices.

As he walked, enveloped by this swarm of memories, Roberto stepped into a puddle and soiled his shoe. Then he started speaking. In a low voice, a whisper, but so precise and articulate that if anyone had been close enough they would have been able to hear distinctly what he was saying.

"You remember the closet where we keep the shoes and all the stuff for cleaning them? I'm seven or eight years old and I'm sitting on the floor in that little room. I'm there to polish my father's shoes. It's something I do every week, polish my father's shoes. There are rules to follow in polishing shoes. First of all, you have to remove the dust, to avoid it getting mixed with the polish and making a disgusting mess. To remove the dust, there's a big light brown brush with hard bristles. Once you've removed all the dust, you can get on with the polishing. You have to apply a little polish and then spread it with a second brush, which is smaller and black with soft bristles, until it's all been absorbed and has even penetrated the stitching. Now the shoe is ready for the most important operation, the buffing. This should be done with a soft cloth and is the pleasantest part of it, because the shoe that was opaque starts to shine – it's transformed in front of your eyes."

A welcoming memory, like when you go to bed in clean, nice-smelling sheets: you're really tired and you know that in a couple of minutes you'll fall asleep and you savour that brief, delicious space of time in which you can huddle in bed and hug the pillow and imagine all kinds of pleasant things, knowing you're safe and secure.

Roberto felt like another cigarette. He'd quit tomorrow, or maybe the day after tomorrow. Or maybe not. Anyway, he wanted to smoke that cigarette in peace, sitting down, savouring the cool late-April night.

Without knowing how he had got there, he realized that he was crossing the park between the Via Flaminia and the Viale Tiziano. He chose a bench in the semi-darkness, some sixty or seventy feet from the all-night flower stall. He sat down, lit a cigarette, smoked it, and then started speaking again.

"Do you remember the living room at home? Outside, it's still dark but the sky is starting to get lighter. I'm sitting on the sofa, ready to go out, and I'm waiting for my father, who's finishing packing his bag, or maybe doing something else; I don't know. I can smell his aftershave in the air. In a while we'll go out and head for the sea. Some beautiful waves are forecast for today. The door is ajar and a light wind blows in

190

from outside and makes the curtains billow in the half-light. I don't know why, but it's those curtains stirred by the wind that bring the tears to my eyes. Then that image disappears and in its place is the shimmer of the sea at sunrise. Seen from a distance, the big waves give the impression that the sea is breathing. We're there, looking down on it, with our surfboards, and our wetsuits already on, and the wind brings us the salt smell of the sea, and in a little while we'll go down to the beach and go into the water."

"Signore?"

And then again, with a touch of impatience: "Signore, is everything all right?"

Roberto looked up in the direction of the voice. The first thing he saw was the Carabinieri symbol on the cap, and beneath it the stripe showing the rank: corporal. Beneath that was the forty-something, scarred face of someone who hadn't been spared acne when he was a boy, with the calm but also somewhat circumspect expression of someone who is familiar with the denizens of the night, knows how to deal with them, and knows that sometimes – not often but sometimes, and you never know when it may happen – they have nasty surprises for you. Behind him, about ten feet away, standing next to a car, a much younger carabiniere.

"Thanks, yes, everything's fine."

"Do you have your papers on you?"

"Yes."

"Do you mind showing them to me?"

"No, I don't mind."

He got out his wallet and was about to show his ID but at the last moment changed his mind. He took out his driving licence and handed it to the corporal.

"Wait here."

"Sure, I'm in no hurry," he said. He felt a strange sensation, as if comforted by waking up with that Carabinieri uniform in front of him. He liked being there, being checked out, on that spring night, waiting for the morning to get under way. He felt lucid, master of the situation. Alert.

The corporal walked away with the licence, reached the car and got in.

They're checking on the computer to find out who I am, he told himself. When they find out, maybe they could tell me. Maybe I'll ask them. The thought cheered him up somehow. He laughed, imagining the corporal's reaction to a question like that. He didn't seem like someone endowed with a sense of humour.

A few minutes later the corporal got out of the car and came back to Roberto, who had lit another cigarette in the meantime.

"Here's your licence, signore. Do you know what time it is?"

"About three?"

"It's almost four. Why are you in the park at this hour, so far from your home? Did something happen to you?"

Did something happen to me? Of course something happened to me. Lots of things have happened to me, but I don't think now is the time to tell you about them.

"No, corporal, thank you. Nothing's ever happened to me. It's just that I couldn't get to sleep and so I came out to have a walk and a bit of a smoke. Now I'm going home. On foot. Long walks relax me." And then, after calculating the time when the men's shift would end, he added, "You two still have a couple of hours left, don't you?"

He stood up from the bench, saluted the carabiniere, who looked at him in surprise, and set off towards home.

Giacomo

Yesterday during break I saw Davide Morandi, my classmate from primary school, who's now in 2C, while I'm in 2D. He's a nice guy, but obsessed with sex: once, in the last year of primary, he got caught by a teacher looking through a porn magazine under his desk. Just before, he'd let me have a quick glance, and I don't think I'd ever seen anything so disgusting.

He asked me if I'd heard anything about videos shot on mobile phones in the toilets of a disco. He said that if you paid it was possible to get a hand job, or more, from some of the girls in the school. You had to see some guys from secondary school who took the money and provided the girls. He said he thought a girl from my class might be involved.

I didn't want to hear any more. I said I didn't know anything about it, that I thought it was a load of bullshit, and that I had to go back to my class anyway.

For the rest of the morning, though, Morandi's words bounced around my head, and a suspicion started growing inside me, something I didn't even have the courage to think about.

Today I tried asking around a bit. The boys didn't have any idea what I was talking about, and anyway – they thought without saying it – I really didn't seem like the kind of person who'd ask questions like that.

Then finally I found someone from the final year of middle school who knew something. Last year our classes went on a school trip together and we became almost friends because we're both crazy about fantasy fiction.

This guy told me there were things going on that it was best not to get into. There were guys older than us involved, real criminals. Apparently, the girls were forced to do what they did, the guys blackmailed them with secretly shot porn videos, and there were also drugs around. In other words, best to steer well clear.

I told him I'd never imagined that things were like that, and thanks for the warning, I'd certainly drop it, so see you, I'm going back to class. Oh, by the way, just out of curiosity, did he happen to know if anybody from my class was involved in any of that stuff? Oh, they did mention that blonde girl, the pretty one, what was her name? Ginevra, maybe? That's the one. See you.

The last hours in class were a nightmare. Ginevra was sitting at her desk, with the same absent expression she's had since she came back to school. As I looked at her, I remembered the disgusting images from that porn magazine I'd peered at two years earlier, and the next thing I thought was that I was in love with her and had to find a way to help her.

In the end I made up my mind: I would talk to her on the way out, I would ask her what was wrong and offer her my help, even though I obviously had no idea what form this help could take.

When the bell rang for the last hour, I had already prepared my rucksack. I was the first out and waited for her to arrive. I started walking just behind her down the corridor, as if it was a chance thing. She didn't notice me until I summoned up the courage to call her by name. It was the first time.

"Ginevra…"

She turned, still walking, and looked at me as if she didn't know me.

"Ginevra… I… the thing is, I wanted to tell you that if… if you need help for any reason… well, I'm here for you, you just have to tell me."

What I was saying was so incoherent, I felt like an idiot the moment I said it. She looked at me a second or two longer, but she wasn't really looking at me, and then she left without even answering.

I was in a real state by the time I got home, wondering what I could do, and I continued wondering all afternoon. A few ideas came into my mind – talk to the teachers, go to the police, stop Ginevra and force her to tell me what was going on – but I ruled them all out because they seemed completely impractical.

I told myself that if my father was still around I'd have been able to talk to him about it and, thinking about my father, I realized the only thing I could really do.

Something obvious. The most obvious thing of all.

I should have thought of it earlier, I know, but when you're a boy it isn't easy to talk to your mother about certain subjects.

25

The telephone rang four or five times before Roberto managed to find it in the kitchen, between the coffee maker, the chipped cups and a half-empty packet of biscuits.

"Hello?"

"Roberto?"

"Emma."

"Hi, everything all right? I'm sorry, but your voice…"

"I'm a bit out of breath, I was doing my exercises…"

"I don't know, I didn't recognize you. Your voice seems… different. But what am I talking about? I only heard you on the phone once, I couldn't even remember your voice." And then, after a moment: "Of course, if I had to wait for you to improve my self-esteem, I'd still be waiting."

"How do you mean?"

"I'm obviously going downhill. In fact, meeting you is a confirmation of my decline. In the past, a man I'd spent an evening with like the one we had would have called me the next morning, at the latest. Even assuming he hadn't kept calling me and asking me to come up and see his apartment. Instead of which, a week has passed, but not a sign of life from you. I'm a former beauty, now it's official."

Roberto did not know what to reply. Of course he had thought of calling her several times, but hadn't been able to bring himself to do so. He had tried asking himself why and couldn't find a good answer. After that night in the doctor's office, everything seemed to be hanging in the air.

"Luckily I've found a reason to phone you. Can you listen to me for a few minutes?" Her voice had become more serious.

"Yes, of course."

"My son Giacomo asked me a strange question."

All at once she seemed to hesitate, as if she had been overcome with doubt about what to say, and maybe about the very advisability of this call. Several seconds passed. Eventually it was Roberto who broke the silence.

"Go on."

"He asked me if I knew any policemen."

"Why did he want to know that?"

"He told me he'd like to speak to a policeman because there's something he has to tell him."

"What kind of thing?"

"He didn't go into detail. All he told me is that a girl in his class is in serious trouble and that it's something the police ought to look into."

"Did he tell you what kind of trouble?"

Emma sighed.

"Giacomo isn't an easy kid. As I said before, talking to him or getting him to talk can be quite complicated. The things he told me, though, seem worrying, if they are true."

A new pause. Silence, apart from her breathing at the other end of the line.

"Listen, you wouldn't have half an hour to spare, would you? We could meet, I could tell you in person, and then maybe you could talk to Giacomo. Talking to him, you'd be able to tell if it's a serious matter or not."

Do I have half an hour? I don't just have half an hour, I have all the time in the world. For months now, I've had all the time in the world and I'll have even more if they throw me out of the Carabinieri. That was what he thought, word for word, but he didn't say it. And yet for the first time the thought of being discharged for good scared him. For a long time he had thought it didn't matter; the idea of abandoning the uniform left him indifferent. Now just the possibility of it dismayed him.

"Yes, I have half an hour. Where shall we meet?"

* * *

This time she was punctual. In fact, she was early, because when Roberto arrived, at three on the dot, she was already there, sitting at the same table as the last time.

When she saw him, Emma stood up, came to him and kissed him on the cheeks. Maybe it was the embrace, maybe it was the two kisses – kisses with the lips on the cheeks, not in the more conventional way, with one cheek pressed against the other – maybe it was something else, but Roberto felt himself go red and a small electrical charge went through his body. He immediately felt embarrassed, irritated with himself for his own awkwardness.

"Thanks for coming," she said.

Don't mention it, it's a pleasure, he was about to reply. But he restrained himself and it seemed to him that he had done the right thing. It was as if he were trying to learn again how to behave, he thought.

"Tell me about Giacomo."

"Yes. Well, the fact is, I don't really know where to begin. Maybe it's just a young boy's imagination and I'm only telling you about it because I want to be reassured."

"Don't worry. Just tell me and we'll try to figure out what to do."

The waitress came and took their orders. Roberto felt good, alert, alive.

"Last night Giacomo asked me if I knew any policemen. I asked him why, and he said there's a girl in his school who's in danger. 'Someone's hurting her and I don't know what to do to help her,' he said."

"What kind of danger?"

"Apparently… apparently some boys the same age, or maybe a bit older, are forcing her to have sex."

"Who's his source?"

He realized he had spoken as if he were in a briefing.

"I mean, how did he find out?"

"He says he heard rumours at school."

"But has he talked to this girl? Did she confide in him, did she tell him something?"

"That's the problem."

"Why?"

"He says she asked him for help, but…"

"But?"

"He says she asked him for help in a dream."

"I'm sorry?"

"That's what he said: the girl asked him for help in a dream. But he sounded so genuine when he told me this that I thought I ought to do something. Then I told myself I did know a policeman, or rather a carabiniere, that having a chat doesn't cost anything, and that I'd feel much calmer if I heard the opinion of a… well, someone like you. I also thought of asking the doctor for advice – we've often talked about Giacomo – but then I thought it was better to call you."

Roberto let a few minutes pass, trying to focus his thoughts, without much success.

"You say they're in the same class?"

"Yes."

"And Giacomo hasn't tried talking to her?"

Emma shrugged and shook her head.

"All right," he said finally, "let me talk to the boy and we'll see what emerges."

"If you like, we can go home now."

"Let's go."

26

The first thing that struck Roberto was the smell. He'd never been good at naming smells – who is? – but there was something sharp and clean in the air you breathed in that apartment.

They entered a living room with a table, a big TV set, a bookcase, fresh flowers in a tall vase made of transparent coloured plastic, a beautiful old leather sofa, prints and photographs in black and white on the walls. Roberto felt a strong desire to belong to what was around him, to be admitted to it, and at the same time he was assailed by a painful awareness of not being up to it, of being for ever excluded.

"Giacomo's in his room. I'll go and fetch him."

Left alone, Roberto found himself doing something he didn't usually do: inspecting the books on the shelves. A few weeks earlier, he wouldn't even have noticed them. Now they aroused his curiosity. He pulled one out, looked at it cautiously, as if it were an object with which he still had to familiarize himself, and then put it back in its place. He did the same thing with another book, then another. He was holding one whose title had attracted his attention – *Heart of Darkness* – when Emma came back into the room. Behind her was a thin young boy with dark eyes. In Roberto's head the apparition of Estela took shape again, sitting on the bed, with the invisible child in the darkness. It lasted a few seconds, like a sudden sharp pain.

"This is Giacomo," Emma said. "Giacomo, this is Roberto."

Roberto held out his hand to the boy and felt it being gripped surprisingly firmly.

"Roberto's a carabiniere."

Then the three of them stood there, saying nothing, until Roberto broke the silence.

"You told me Giacomo wanted to talk to me. Maybe it'd be easier if we were alone for a few minutes. If you don't mind."

Emma looked around, dumbfounded, searching for something to say but not finding it. Then she shrugged, told them to call her when they were finished, and left the room.

Roberto looked at the boy, and the boy sustained his gaze.

"Shall we sit down?"

They both sat down on the sofa. Roberto felt the cracks in the leather beneath his hands and was surprised at the way all his senses – touch, at this particular moment – were coming back to life.

"I don't think you're the kind of person who beats about the bush," Roberto said.

"So you're a carabiniere?"

He'd been right.

"Yes, I'm a marshal."

"What do you do exactly?"

"I'm a detective, I deal with organized crime." No point being too specific, like saying that he *used to* deal with organized crime but would never be doing so again.

The answer didn't seem to impress the boy.

"How do you know my mother?"

"Her car broke down once, I saw her, stopped and helped her to get it started. Then we happened to meet again. We've chatted a few times. Today she called me and told me you'd asked to speak to a policeman or a carabiniere. I think I'm the only person she knows in that line of work, that's why she turned to me."

The boy scratched his head: he had exhausted the preliminaries and did not know how to carry on.

201

"From what your mother told me, you know something about a problem a school friend of yours has."

"Yes."

"Do you want to tell me about it?"

Giacomo told his story, and he did so in a brief, precise way, in the tone of an officer reporting on an investigation. There was a rumour doing the rounds at school about a pornography and prostitution ring. Apparently, it was run by a group of older boys, maybe from high school. There were girls forced to have sex and let themselves be filmed, and among them was a classmate of his – Giacomo told him her name – who was desperately in need of help.

"Who told you these things?"

"People from school, but I don't know any of their names," he said, touching his face in the kind of gesture common in those not telling the whole truth. It doesn't matter, Roberto thought. The boy was protecting his sources. Like any self-respecting detective.

"Have you tried to talk about it with the girl – Ginevra you told me her name was, right?"

"I tried."

"And what did she say?"

"Nothing."

"So how can you be so sure she's involved with this ring and needs help?"

Giacomo hesitated before replying.

"I know you're going to think this is crazy, but I had a dream. And in that dream Ginevra asked for help. She was desperate."

Actually, even though he didn't say so, Roberto didn't really think it was crazy at all. In fact, without even realizing it, he started to react like a carabiniere and to think about what he might be able to do. Maybe because – dream or no dream – rumours like that needed to be checked out anyway. When there are stories circulating that won't go away, the likeliest explanation is that they contain at least some truth. All the best investigations come out of rumours that won't go away.

It struck him he might be able to stand outside the school, have Giacomo point out the girl to him, take a look at her, see where she went and then, on the basis of what emerged – if anything did emerge – play it by ear. Improvise. As he had always done. With all the free time he had, what did it cost him? Worst case scenario, it would all amount to nothing.

"All right, Giacomo. I'm going to look into this, but I need your help."

"What do I have to do?"

"What time do you leave school tomorrow?"

"One o'clock."

"At one o'clock tomorrow I'll be standing outside your school. When you come out, try to stand close to this girl so that I know which one she is. When you see me, make sure I've understood who the girl is – I'll give you a sign – and then just go home. I'll see to the rest. Oh, and, of course, don't tell anyone about this conversation of ours. Agreed?"

Giacomo said all right and then sat there looking at him, as if something were still hanging in the air.

"Is there anything else you want to tell me?"

"Yes."

"Go ahead."

"Thank you."

"Why are you thanking me?"

"For listening to me and not treating me like a child."

Roberto made a sign with his head that was like a bow, a gesture of respect.

"I think we should call your mother now. See you tomorrow outside school at one o'clock. All right?"

"All right."

They called Emma. When she came back in she said nothing, but her face was full of questions.

27

An hour later Roberto was with the doctor. It seemed as if months had passed since the last time.

"I don't know what to talk about today."

"Then don't talk about anything."

"I feel… I can't really say how I feel."

"Maybe a bit uncomfortable?"

"Yes, maybe."

"It's a new situation – it's normal you should feel like this."

"Is it because of what I told you last time?"

"It's because of several things, including what we told each other last time. Overall, it was rather an atypical session."

Roberto rubbed his face with his hands.

"You said it's a new situation, didn't you?"

"Yes."

"Do you know something?"

"What?"

"I have the impression that all at once words – I mean normal words that I knew perfectly, like *situation* – have a clearer, more precise meaning."

"That's because the world is starting to make sense again. And in case it wasn't clear: that's good news."

"Does that mean I'm getting better?"

"Yes, I'd say it does mean you're getting better. In the next few days we'll start reducing the dosage of the medication."

"I'm sorry about what you told me last time… about your son."

The doctor gave a little smile.

"I shouldn't say this because it's completely against the rules, but talking to you about him did me a lot of good."

*　*　*

At the door, the doctor shook his hand and said he was pleased with the way things were going.

"I've met a patient of yours," Roberto said. "A woman."

"I know."

"I assumed you did."

"I think it's a good thing."

Roberto stood there looking at him.

"A good thing," the doctor repeated, then smiled, said goodbye, and went back inside.

*　*　*

The next morning, he woke up in a changeable mood: a mixture of joy and slight anxiety. He did some exercise, took a shower, and then dressed, paying attention to what he was putting on, trying to concentrate on every single movement. Starting with the trousers, first one leg then the other, keeping his balance without looking for something to hold on to; taking a shirt he had ironed over the weekend, feeling smug for a few seconds because the ironing had been done well, putting first one arm and then the other in; sitting down on the edge of the bed and going on to the socks, after making sure they matched and didn't have any holes; trying on the new shoes he had bought a few days earlier; doing up the belt and realizing he could push it to a hole he had never used; putting on the jacket, with a final glance in the mirror.

It was absurd, he thought, but he had liked getting dressed.

Maybe because he had done it with due care and attention? He opened his wallet, took out his ID and looked at it as if he had never seen it before. Obviously the question was the photograph. It wasn't actually all that old, but it looked like someone else. Who was this guy in uniform, without a beard, without deep lines on his forehead and with the cool gaze of someone who's afraid of nothing? At what moment had he disappeared to give way to someone else? Where was he now? Because he must be somewhere, maybe in a parallel world to which you just had to find the door, Roberto thought, taking an unreasonable and beneficial comfort from this absurd thought.

He left home with the joy and anxiety whirling around together, and went and had breakfast in the bar where he had twice met Emma. He had a cappuccino and a croissant, smoked a single cigarette and watched the people passing, enjoying the idleness for the first time in longer than he could remember.

It was a bright morning, but not hot. A perfect spring day, Roberto thought as he walked, calm and alert, looking around him, *seeing* what was around. Getting his eyes back in working order.

A few minutes before one he was outside the school.

* * *

The angry growl of the bell could even be heard on the street. About thirty seconds passed, thirty seconds of suspense during which it seemed as if the sound had had no effect, and then the children started pouring out of the building. Giacomo appeared almost immediately, walking next to a blonde girl, staying close to her until his eyes met Roberto's. Then he stopped, with the slightly dismayed expression of someone who has performed his task and has no possibility of influencing what will happen next. Even if he wanted to.

One moment you're indispensable, the next you're irrelevant. Roberto looked at him and guessed what he must be feeling. Then he turned and set off.

Ginevra was walking fast, glancing behind her every now and again. She came to a bus stop and joined the small crowd that was waiting. Roberto approached. Several buses stopped and left again. Then one arrived and the girl got on, and Roberto got on behind her. He didn't have a ticket. If they stop me I'll show my ID, he told himself. On the bus Roberto studied the girl. Pretty, but nothing amazing.

Ginevra got off after three stops, walked for a few more minutes, reached a posh-looking apartment block, opened the front door with a key and disappeared inside.

Roberto checked the names by the bells, to make sure this was where the girl lived. The surname Giacomo had given him was there. Just to respect the rules of surveillance, he waited on the opposite pavement for half an hour. In that half-hour only one elderly lady entered the building and nobody came out. It was about two when Roberto decided it was time to go.

28

"Emma?"

"Roberto."

"Er… how are you?"

"Fine, and you?"

"Fine. I went to Giacomo's school."

"Yes, he told me. Did you… did you find out anything?"

"I followed the girl home, but nothing happened."

"Roberto?' She had lowered her voice.

"Yes?"

"What do you think of this story?"

Pause. Roberto did not know what to think. Not yet, at least.

"Roberto, are you there?"

"I don't know. I'll go back to the school tomorrow and see what happens. If anything happens."

Emma was silent for a while, then: "Will you call me afterwards?"

"Of course I will."

Another silence. Was she asking him to call her only because she wanted to be informed about what had happened? Or was there another reason?

"Say hello to Giacomo for me. Tell him I'm dealing with it."

"He'll be pleased. He liked you. That doesn't happen often."

* * *

The following morning passed in the same way, at the same contradictory rhythm, both lazy and active. For no very clear reason, Roberto had brought a small pair of binoculars and a camera with him. They were unlikely to be needed, but taking them didn't cost anything, he had told himself as he left home with an old khaki bag over his shoulder, feeling slightly ridiculous.

Giacomo came out of school almost running, and slowed down when he saw Roberto. They exchanged a rapid glance. Then the boy turned and went away.

Immediately afterwards, Ginevra came out and the sequence was identical to that of the day before. Bus ride, getting off, a short stretch on foot, going into the building.

Roberto waited outside for a while, starting to feel stupid. What the hell was he doing? Why this ridiculous private investigation, like an amateur sleuth with his bag over his shoulder? He left, suddenly worried that someone might see him and ask him what he was doing there.

By the time he got home, he had decided he would make one last attempt, and then that would be it. If nothing happened, maybe he would refer the thing to his colleagues and let them deal with it. Assuming there was anything to deal with.

* * *

The next day he arrived slightly late, just in time to see the girl come out of school and hurry off in the direction of the bus stop. As he already knew the destination, Roberto kept himself at a greater distance, in such a way as to have a broader vision and – he thought – also to avoid anyone noticing him, a middle-aged man of somewhat dubious appearance following a schoolgirl.

The stream of kids and adults was the same as the two previous days. Roberto, though, thought he noted, in the regular movement of the people, a discontinuity, an element that didn't fit the rhythm.

A detective's instinct goes in search of the jarring note and sees what escapes others: small objects that are missing or in the wrong place, slightly odd postures, forced gestures, slight breathlessness, blushing, elusive glances or others that linger too long. Someone who's somewhere he shouldn't be; someone going slowly who should be going fast or going fast when he should be going slowly; someone who looks around and seems to be looking at nothing; excessive talkativeness or silence. An alteration in a routine. You concentrate on unusual details instead of letting yourself be distracted by the apparent normality of the overall picture.

In some ways a good detective is like a good doctor. In both cases it is a matter of having an eye for details that other people don't spot.

In that flow of people – adults, but above all kids – there was an element of irregularity that Roberto perceived as a phenomenon, as an alteration of the whole, even before he identified the cause.

The cause was a boy of about fifteen, unusually muscular for his age, who was walking fast and looking straight ahead.

He was walking as if he were following someone, Roberto told himself, all at once feeling his heart starting to beat more quickly and the instinct of the chase reawakening, intact and primeval.

They got to the stop just as the bus that the girl had taken two days previously was leaving. She tried to catch up with it but couldn't. So she stood a little aside, close to a front door. Roberto kept his distance. He had lost sight of the muscular boy, then spotted him as he too arrived at the stop and looked around. Then a group of Africans got in the way and prevented him from following the scene. He went closer, and when he was about thirty feet away he saw the muscular boy standing next to Ginevra. A little further on, there was another. He looked older but seemed less solid and less dangerous than the first one. Leaders and followers. It always works like that, and age almost never has anything to do with it.

The muscular boy was talking, and the girl was shaking her head, but weakly, as if resigned. After a while, the other boy seemed to point at something. Ginevra tried to look away, and the muscular boy took her chin between his fingers and forced her to look somewhere else. At that moment another bus arrived. The girl made an attempt to get on it, but the boy barred her way and stopped her.

The second boy was keeping an eye on the situation. When Roberto saw him looking in his direction, he pretended to be looking in a shop window, counted to five and then again turned. The three of them had moved, the leader walking beside Ginevra, the other boy a few steps behind.

Roberto set off after them, trying to maintain a safe distance. The muscular boy made a call on his mobile as he walked. They didn't look round again, but all the same, after a while Roberto took off his jacket, pulled his shirt out of his trousers and became another person. Soon afterwards, the three met up with a thin, anaemic-looking boy in glasses. Without a word, he joined the group.

Roberto followed them for seven or eight minutes until they came to the front door of a building. The leader had the keys. He opened and they all disappeared inside, closing the door behind them.

The first thing to do was get inside that building, Roberto told himself. Any other problem he would solve as it came up. There was the brass plate of a law firm on the door. Roberto rang the bell. A nasal, heavily accented female voice replied rudely.

"Carabinieri. Open up, we have to serve a summons."

There was only a brief hesitation, then the lock buzzed like a hornet and the door opened. Roberto ran to the lift: the red light was still on and the car still in motion. It stopped on the fifth floor, the top floor of the building.

Waiting for the lift would make him waste too much time, Roberto thought. He ran up the stairs, two steps at a time, and by the time he reached the fifth floor his heart was throbbing like a piston. There were two doors on the landing and neither of them had a name on it. Trying to catch his breath, he rang the bell to his left. When it was opened – and depending on *who* opened it – he would decide what to do.

About a minute passed. Roberto had the distinct impression that someone was looking at him through the peephole. Then he heard a somewhat shaky elderly male voice.

"Who is it?"

"Carabinieri, signore. I need to ask you a few questions, could you please open the door?"

"A carabiniere? What do you want with me?"

"I just need to ask you a few questions. Would you mind opening?"

"And how do I know you're really a carabiniere and not a criminal?"

"I'll show you my ID, signore," Roberto said, trying to control a touch of exasperation in his voice. "Can you see it through the peephole?"

"Let's see," the old man said, his tone filled with suspicion.

Roberto held the ID at the level of the peephole. Several more seconds passed, then from inside he heard a noise of locks and bolts, and at last the door opened. A very old man appeared, without any hair and with unusually smooth pink skin.

The most unusual thing about the image that presented itself to Roberto, however, was not the man's appearance.

It was the fact that the man had a big revolver in his hand.

"Don't worry about this. If you're really a carabiniere I won't need it. If you aren't, and that ID is fake, you still have time to leave. The photo doesn't look much like you."

"Is that gun loaded, signore?" Roberto said, trying to get over his surprise.

"Of course it's loaded, what a question. And if you really are a carabiniere, I'd like you to know I have a licence for it."

"I don't doubt that, signore. The ID is genuine, though the photo's a few years old and I've changed a bit since then. I'd be very grateful to you if you could lower your gun. I just need to know who lives in the apartment next door."

The old man looked at him with a strangely surprised and satisfied expression. The barrel of the gun was lowered, and the old man moved aside and gestured to Roberto to come in.

"At last you've taken notice. A lot of the phone calls were from me. You took your time but at last you've taken notice."

He moved back inside, giving a cautious smile. The apartment was dark and stank of mothballs. Roberto had no idea what the old man meant but thought it was best not to tell him that.

"That's always the way, signore. Unfortunately we have a lot of work, and it's hard to keep track of everything. Can you tell me who lives in that apartment?"

The old man explained. The apartment belonged to a lawyer who had gone to live there after separating from his wife. Then he had found a new partner and had moved to her house. Now the apartment was used by his son, who was a delinquent, and his friends, who were delinquents like him. They came there often and played loud music at all hours of the day and night, shouting and yelling and drinking.

"Drugs too, if you ask me," the old man concluded laconically.

Roberto seized the opportunity.

"As it happens, signore, we've had a tip-off that a group of young men are using and maybe also dealing narcotics in an apartment in this building. That's what I've come to check."

"But do you do this kind of job alone? Shouldn't there be a group of you, a patrol?"

213

The man was old but not gaga. Roberto felt like laughing, but tried to reply appropriately.

"Of course, signore, actually there are three of us. My colleagues are outside in the street, to stop anyone escaping and to catch the drugs if they try to throw them out of the windows or off the balconies. That's what dealers often try and do when there's a raid: they get rid of the drugs by throwing them out into the street. Now, signore, I'd like to ask for your help in order to proceed."

Apparently convinced, the old man stuck the gun into the belt of his trousers and then looked at Roberto with a determined, expectant expression. His face was saying that now he was prepared to cooperate. It struck Roberto that this was one of the most comical situations he had ever come across in his career.

"Go on."

"Do you by any chance have a balcony, on the inside, that adjoins the balcony of the next apartment?"

"Yes, of course."

"Would you mind showing it to me?"

"What do you want to do?"

"I'd like to go from one balcony to the other in order to get inside that other apartment and take them by surprise. As I'm sure you'll understand, if I knock at the door there's a risk they'll get rid of the drugs, maybe by flushing them down the toilet."

It was a convincing explanation. The old man asked Roberto to follow him and led him through the apartment, with the stink of mothballs becoming ever stronger, as far as the internal balcony. The balconies were adjoining and it would be very easy to climb over the railing and go from one to the other. There were no bars or shutters on the windows. And the glass seemed normal, not shatterproof or anything like that. It would be easy to break.

The old man was happy to cooperate now, but maintained a vigilant attitude. He was anything but gaga, Roberto thought.

"Don't you need a search warrant?"

"Usually, yes, signore. But in cases of emergency – and this is a case of emergency – we can search premises on our own initiative, as laid down by article 103 of the code on narcotics. Naturally we have to request ratification from the prosecutor later."

"But don't you have a gun?"

Another good question. I don't have one because they took it away from me. They told me I'm almost mad and that's why they took it away from me. Now I don't have a gun and in all probability, given what I'm about to do, I'll never have one again.

"No, signore, sometimes when we raid a premises we prefer not to carry weapons to avoid the risk of their going off accidentally. In this case we seem to be dealing with minors, so our operational protocol doesn't allow the use of firearms."

Operational protocol. He certainly hadn't lost the knack for talking bullshit.

The old man told him to proceed, but to be careful because it could be dangerous.

Yes, it could be dangerous. For a few moments Roberto, who had never suffered from dizziness in his life, was seized with a touch of panic which – he realized immediately – could grow and paralyse him. You're forty-seven years old, was the last thing he told himself before climbing over, walking a few feet on the outside, holding on to the rail, then climbing over again and landing on the other balcony with his heart apparently about to leap out of his throat.

He looked inside. There was nobody in that particular room, but music was playing at high volume somewhere in the apartment – house music of some kind – and the pane of glass was vibrating to the throb of it.

Roberto rolled his jacket into a ball and, using it to protect his hand, struck a single sharp but almost delicate blow. The glass broke around his fist, only as much as was necessary, and almost noiselessly – not that the noise would have been heard over the booming of the music anyway. He slipped his hand through the hole, opened the window and went in without thinking. He would decide what to do and say depending on what he found. He walked down a long, dark, bare corridor, guided by the relentless rhythm of the music.

29

When Roberto entered the bedroom, he found what he had vaguely been expecting. The girl and the third boy to show up were on the bed. The other two were filming with their phones, from different angles, as if they were shooting a film according to rudimentary but specific directions.

In reality, Roberto would later be unable to recount with certainty what he saw at that precise moment. In his memories, those perceived images would become mixed with those seen soon afterwards in the videos: a revolting, distressing, pitiless intertwining of undeveloped bodies.

"Carabinieri!" he yelled in order to be heard over the booming of the music. It was the third time in just a few minutes, after such a long interval. "Put your phones on the floor. You, get off the bed, and all of you get on your knees with your faces to the wall and your hands behind your heads."

The muscular boy tried to brazen it out.

"What the fuck do you want? Who are you? This is a private apartment, my father's a lawyer and a friend of —"

Roberto went up to him and slapped him across the face.

"Turn off this fucking music and get down on your knees with your face against the wall and your hands behind your head. You two do the same and don't make me repeat myself another time, or I'll really get pissed off."

The lawyer's son appeared to be on the verge of saying something. Then he saw Roberto's eyes and thought better of it. He threw the mobile phone on the floor, switched off the stereo behind him and then got down on his knees by the wall. The one who was on the bed stood up, naked from the waist down. His face was smooth, but his genitals were as hairy as a man's. He put on his trousers, tripping over. He seemed like a little boy about to burst into tears, and he too went and knelt facing the wall. The third one had remained on his feet, motionless, almost paralysed, with the expression of someone who is only just realizing the enormity of the situation he has got himself into. Roberto looked at him and nodded. The gesture woke him up, and he handed over the phone and knelt next to the other two.

The silence that had suddenly taken the place of that deafening music made the situation even more unreal. The girl was on the bed, trying to get dressed. Her body was the mysterious, heart-rending combination of two creatures: a woman and a child. Roberto's feelings were in turmoil. Anger, sorrow, protectiveness, the urge to cry, violence that emerged in fits and starts and had to be kept under control. And lost pride. The pride of someone who has arrived late – you always arrive late – but not *too* late. He saw again the faces of those young Mexican girls so many years earlier, and it occurred to him that he was settling an old account.

"Your name's Ginevra, isn't it?" he asked her when she was covered enough to be able to respond.

The girl couldn't open her mouth, just looked at him in terror, like a trapped animal.

"Finish getting dressed, go out there and wait for me."

She obeyed. She left the room without looking at anything or anybody, her eyes lost in a void full of monsters that the others could not see.

The one who had previously been on the bed started sobbing.

"I didn't mean to do anything wrong. Forgive me, I didn't mean to do anything wrong. Let me go – if my mother hears about this she'll kill me. I'm sorry, I'm sorry. They told me it was normal, that they'd already done it lots of times. She agreed to it, she took the money and —"

"Shut up, arsehole," said the muscular boy, who was clearly the leader and already a hardened criminal.

"No, *you* shut up," Roberto cut in, "and don't let me hear another word from you. If I hear you talking without my permission, I'll tear your head off. Is that clear?"

It was clear.

Roberto quickly searched the boys. In the leader's pockets he found another two mobile phones, a few hundred euros, a hard rubber baton and two bunches of keys.

"Don't move and don't talk, any of you," he said, and walked out of the bedroom into the corridor, where Ginevra stood, pathetically out of place like a small, unhappy scarecrow. Roberto led her into the kitchen, told her to wait in there, and closed the door of the apartment with the key he had taken from the leader, just in case the boys got it into their heads to try and escape.

He glanced at the videos in the phones, but they made him so sick he decided there was no need to watch any further.

He let a minute pass, thinking about what he ought to say, and then phoned Carella.

"Roberto, great to hear from you," Carella said, in the affectionate but at the same time not entirely genuine tone of someone talking to a sick friend who needs to be treated with kindness and circumspection. "So you finally called me. How are you?"

"Fine, thanks. Are you on duty?"

"Of course, why?"

"Then you need to get a couple of cars and some of your people and join me as quickly as you can. I've come across a little cesspit."

There were a few seconds of silence at the other end. Roberto gave Carella time to come round to the idea that this call was strictly business and that the man on the phone might again be the man he had known in his previous life.

"Can you give me a few more details?"

"Gang rape, prostitution of minors, kidnapping. A nasty business involving kids. Bring along a female colleague, to take care of the victim."

"How did you get involved in all this?"

"How about I tell you everything in person? It's best if you take over as soon as possible. The sooner you get here, the better."

Once again Roberto imagined his colleague's mental activity, the many questions he must be asking himself. He waited. In the end Carella said all right, just let him get a team together and he'd be right there.

The tone of his voice was different now.

30

He tried to talk to the girl, but there was only one thing on her mind.

"Can I go now?"

"Of course, in a little while I'll make sure somebody takes you home."

"No, thanks, I can go by myself."

That "No, thanks" brought a pang to his heart. Roberto had to make an effort to hold back his emotions, as well as any questions about what had happened and how it had started, and why. Those kinds of questions were someone else's job.

"All right, we'll see what we can do, you just have to be a little patient."

And then, after a pause, lying and feeling ashamed of himself: "In a little while, you'll be able to go back home, even alone, if you prefer."

"But I have to go now. If it gets too late my parents start to worry."

"Keep calm, we'll inform your parents."

But she wasn't calm. She wasn't calm at all, because gradually the situation was becoming clearer in her head.

"You're not going to tell them…" She couldn't find the words. "Please let me go home."

Roberto would have liked to give her a hug and tell her not to worry, that her parents would understand and would help her, and that the world was not inhabited only by people like those three, or those two, or all those – God knows how many – who had handled her body.

Except that of course he couldn't give her a hug and he wouldn't even have the courage to give her any guarantees on how the world was populated, or on what her parents and all the others would understand.

"Don't worry, there won't be any problem with your parents. In a very short time you'll go home and everything will be over."

And then, thank goodness, Carella arrived with four other carabinieri, three men and a woman. They had been really quick, even though it seemed to Roberto that an interminable length of time had passed. Apart from Carella, the others were young, and there was something about their way of moving, of behaving, of occupying the space, that gave Roberto the clear sensation that he himself belonged to another time.

From that moment, things moved much more quickly.

Roberto explained what had happened. He told almost the whole truth, remaining vague only about the source of his information. He alluded to an informant inside the school but didn't give any further details. His colleagues were professionals – you don't ask a professional for details about his informant – and didn't ask any questions.

The young woman carabiniere took charge of Ginevra and led her away. She seemed to know what she was doing, and Roberto felt relieved at that.

The others dealt with the boys. The one caught on the bed with the girl was still crying, the second one had a large dark patch on his trousers and stank of urine, and the leader was very pale. He was still putting on airs and trying to act in a way he thought appropriate to his role, but he too seemed on the verge of breaking down.

Carella informed the deputy prosecutor at the juvenile court. He said he had received an urgent and extremely reliable tip-off about the presence of a large quantity of drugs inside that apartment, and that he had proceeded to search it for drugs – on the basis of the very rule that Roberto had mentioned to the old man with the revolver – and had come across something more serious than a simple case of drug dealing.

When he had finished talking on the phone, he turned to Roberto.

"So, Marshal Marías, you're back at last?"

Roberto shrugged his shoulders and gave an embarrassed smile. Carella smiled too.

"Do you want to sign the documents? We need to find a way to justify your presence here, but we'll think up something. This may be a good omen. When you get back on the force you can come and work with us."

"No, let's not cause needless problems. I'm going now. Maybe later we'll talk on the phone and you can tell me what develops."

Carella did not insist.

"All right, when we've finished I'll call you."

* * *

When Carella called, late that evening, his voice sounded tired.

"We've finished now. The next time you come across something like this, please call the police."

Then he told him how it had gone. Luckily, the deputy prosecutor was on the ball and had immediately ordered the boys' homes to be searched. The result had been what might have been expected: porn videos and photos, hashish, a whole lot of money, and actual if rudimentary accounts with the names of the clients – all aged between thirteen and sixteen – the amounts paid, the services received. The three boys had been questioned that same afternoon and had confessed everything, or at least enough to reconstruct the modus operandi of the gang and identify the other members.

The girls were approached in discos or at private parties, the sexual acts – sometimes consensual, sometimes not – were filmed, and then the videos were used to blackmail them into prostituting themselves.

"How's the girl?"

"So-so. Her parents are taking her out of that school – that's obvious – but it'll take time for her to recover. Some of the videos we've found are pretty disgusting."

"Go to bed, you sound terrible."

"I'm going now. Oh, obviously there's no mention of your name in any of the paperwork. You were never in that apartment."

31

The door opened immediately, and by the time Roberto got to Emma's apartment she was waiting for him in the entrance. A day had gone by.

"Come in, Giacomo's still with his grandparents," she said, her expression a mixture of anxiety and a touch of surprised admiration. "Would you like a coffee?"

They had coffee in the kitchen and Roberto told her everything he had only hinted at over the phone. When he had finished, Emma stood up, opened the window, picked up an ashtray and asked for a cigarette. After giving it to her, Roberto lit one for himself. He did it slowly, almost as if he wanted to be conscious of every single moment, to stamp it in his memory.

"I think I'm going to quit tomorrow."

Emma looked at him as if she hadn't heard.

"How did Giacomo know what was happening?"

Roberto stubbed out his cigarette, breaking it as he did so, and shifted on his chair.

"What do you mean?"

"How did he know? Please tell me he wasn't involved."

Roberto looked at her in surprise. He hadn't immediately grasped the reason for the question. "What are you talking about? Of course he wasn't involved. We already talked about it: there were rumours about all this at school and he heard them, like everyone else. Maybe in the toilets, maybe someone boasted or one of the girls blurted something out." And then he added: "Maybe it was actually Ginevra who confided in him to get it off her chest. Who knows? Right now it doesn't matter anyway. The important thing is that everything has… resolved itself. So to speak."

"And why did he tell you that story about the dream if he had nothing to hide?"

"Because maybe he really did dream that she was asking for help. Through the dream, his unconscious was telling him he had to *do* something. Why don't you ask the doctor what he thinks?"

She looked him in the eyes for a long time. "I already have," she said at last. "I phoned him before you arrived."

"And what did he say?"

"The same as you."

Roberto tried to appear nonchalant, but without much success.

"How did you find the place? How did you happen to get there just at that moment?"

"Oh, a bit of professional skill, a bit of luck."

"Luck? Bullshit, luck doesn't exist and you're a strange man, signor detective. There are a whole lot of things you ought to tell me, never mind about luck."

You're wrong, Roberto thought, luck definitely does exist. And bad luck too, while we're about it.

At that moment Giacomo arrived. Roberto stood up to shake his hand. Emma looked at the two of them, said she was going to have a shower, and disappeared.

"You know what happened, don't you?"

The boy nodded, looking Roberto straight in the eyes, just as his mother had done a few minutes earlier.

"People will take care of her now. Of course she'll be changing school. It'll take time, but she'll get over it."

Actually, Roberto didn't know if the girl would get over it.

Nobody knows in cases like that. But it seemed to him that Giacomo had the right to hear him say these things.

"You were the one who saved her," he added.

Giacomo continued to look at him and Roberto became aware of the incredible melancholy in those eyes, which were so similar to his mother's.

"I'm very sad," Giacomo said.

"Why?"

"Because I'll never see her again."

Roberto made an effort to swallow. Then, without even realizing what he was doing, he went to Giacomo and gave him a quick hug.

"See you again maybe," he said, after a few moments, when they had separated.

"I'd like that," the boy replied simply.

Then he got up and went out, leaving those last words hanging in the air and Roberto sitting in the kitchen as it got darker.

Giacomo

For at least two hours I listened to the collection I made for Ginevra and will never give her. It finished and then I started it again from the beginning, and then again and again, and it seemed to me that all the words and all the notes of the songs had a special meaning created just for me.

It's strange how the same thing – listening to music – can be something you really like and at the same time something that really hurts you.

Only a few days have passed since the last time I wrote in this diary and it seems as if years have passed.

Even after taking the decision it wasn't easy to talk to my mother, for a whole lot of reasons. Among others, I was almost certain she wouldn't take me seriously.

But that's not how it went. She listened to me – really listened, without that unbearable attitude that adults some-times have – in other words, she didn't treat me like a child.

It was a surprise, and one thing really amazed me: when I asked her if she could put me in touch with a policeman she didn't object and said she would try to introduce me to a friend of hers who was a carabiniere. I was amazed that she had a friend who was a carabiniere, but of course I said yes and the next day she brought him home.

He was different from the way I'd imagined a carabiniere. I don't know if I can explain it properly, but I immediately liked him. He seemed like the kind of person you would like to be friends with even though he's a man of more than forty and you're a boy of almost twelve.

I know I'm saying something absurd but in a way Roberto – that's his name – reminded me of Scott.

Roberto must be really good at his job, because in only three days he found out what was happening to Ginevra and arrested three guys, a pupil from my school who's been repeating a year and two older boys who went to secondary school.

I say *went*, because now I think they'll have to attend school in juvenile prison. Even though, to tell the truth, I don't know how these things work and maybe they'll come out soon and be able to go back to a normal school.

Ginevra will also change schools and I don't think I'll ever see her again.

The thought of going into class every day and not seeing her makes my heart burst with sadness. This thing about sadness bursting is a phrase I heard in a song and I can't find a better way to say how I feel.

* * *

It was several nights since I'd last seen Scott and I realized I won't be dreaming about him any more.

Then it occurred to me that if he was created by my imagination, I could ask my imagination to let me see him one last time and say goodbye. Even without sleeping.

So I lowered the blind, lay down on the bed, closed my eyes, and concentrated with all my might.

After a while I succeeded, and Scott appeared. He was sitting there, calm and serious, beside my bed.

"Hi, Scott, it's good to have you here."

It's nice to see you too, chief.

"We're saying goodbye, aren't we?"

I'm afraid so, chief.

"Why? Why can't we still see each other in the park, at least once in a while?"

You don't need me any more, chief. My task is complete.

Those words made me angry. I wanted to tell him that it was one of the stupidest things I'd ever heard. Who gave a damn about the task? Couldn't we still see each other just for the pleasure of being together, of running in the park, of swimming in that lake with the turquoise water? Why did everything have to have a reason and a purpose?

That wasn't what I said.

"I'll never see you again and I'll never see Ginevra again. I'm so sad." I was sniffing, trying hard not to burst into tears.

You did what needed to be done, chief. I'm proud of you and your father would be too.

I sniffed again, but that sentence had sent a quiver through me and made me feel better.

"When I have another dog I'll call him Scott – you know that, don't you?"

I felt him lick my hand, but he didn't say anything.

"Scott, did you hear me?"

He didn't answer me.

Then I opened my eyes and saw that he had gone away for ever.

32

The car was moving slowly, so that they wouldn't miss the badly signposted turn-off for the beach. The sky was becoming lighter, and through the lowered windows a sharp breeze came in, penetrating their light clothes and making them shiver. It was bound to be hot later, but right now the air was still cool and sharp. It was the perfect moment that precedes the arrival of certain summer days.

Emma was driving and Roberto was looking at the road. He was aware of the changes inside and outside himself; he registered them, and let them happen. Just as the doctor had taught him. Images from his past – or maybe sometimes from his imagination – succeeded one another, passed by and disappeared. Every now and again a wave of fear arrived, but it passed quickly and turned into a kind of tingling of the soul.

They had left Rome very early, to be at the sea before the sun rose. The forecasts had said storms at sea. Santa Marinella isn't Dana Point, but that day there would be some very large waves. Exceptionally large for the Tyrrhenian Sea and for the month of July.

Together with the waves, an extraordinary influx of surfers was predicted, so it was vital to get there very early, or else the beach would be too crowded and the sea impracticable.

They parked in an open space where there were already a few cars. Roberto had the feeling that his strength was abandoning him completely. He had the impression he was moving laboriously, almost in slow motion. He got out of the car and stood there, motionless, unsure what to do.

"Are you planning to go in the water fully dressed?" Emma said, a mixture of irony and apprehension in her voice. Maybe she was wondering if this had been a good idea. The last time this man had surfed had been more than thirty years earlier. What was there to say he'd be able to do so again? He turned his gaze towards the sea. It was an expanse of foam, illuminated by the pale, uniform light of dawn.

Without saying anything, Roberto got back in the car to change. He came out in his bathing trunks, an old T-shirt and old blue-and-white tennis shoes. He took the surfboard from the roof rack, put it under his arm and looked at Emma.

"Roberto, if you don't feel up to it…" The hint of irony had disappeared.

"Let's go," he said, and they walked towards the sea.

On the beach they glimpsed a few boys and a few surfboards planted upright in the sand. Nobody seemed to have gone into the water yet. A north-westerly wind was blowing, not too strong, but dry and full of dangerous promise.

You won't make it, Roberto said to himself as they walked down onto the beach. That feeling of sluggishness wouldn't let go of him.

There's no way you're going to make it. You're old and you've forgotten how. How old were you the last time? When *was* the last time? You can't even remember. Did that period ever exist? It's not just remote, it's in another world. Would you be able to say how you can tell memories from dreams? Those waves you remember are silent, just like dreams. So maybe they aren't real.

You won't make it.

What was that sentence the doctor had quoted? It's one thing to wait for the wave, another to get up on the board when it arrives. Precisely.

Emma was walking behind him. For a very long moment, Roberto thought – really *believed* – that she was his mother and he had the impression he was in another place and in another life that could have been and hadn't been.

The wind again carried the salt smell. The same as so many years before. He took off his shoes. His feet sank into the cool sand. On his face, on his body, on the surfboard, he felt the eyes of the boys who had already taken over the beach. Gazes first of hostility, then, after getting a proper look at him – an old man – full of scorn.

One of the boys stood up and took a few steps towards him. Maybe he wanted to tell him something. Maybe he wanted to tell him that this beach, at least at this time of the day, was their property. It was their place, not his. Or maybe he didn't want to tell him anything and had stood up only to stretch his legs. What was certain is that the boy's eyes and Roberto's met just as the sun was rising. Then the boy looked away and decided to turn back and forget about whatever it was he had thought of doing.

He sat down again on the sand, near the boards, exchanging embarrassed jokes with his friends, laughing a bit louder than necessary, making sure he was heard.

But Roberto did not hear him. He stopped for just a few seconds to listen to the roar of the waves. The sun was rising behind him, casting his long shadow onto the beach, as far as the water and down into the sea.

At that moment, as he was looking at his shadow mixing with the foam, he remembered something he had read years before.

In the early Nineties a merchant ship carrying a cargo of toys from Hong Kong to the United States was caught in a terrible storm. Thanks to the very high waves, a dozen containers ended up in the water and broke open, spilling into the ocean tens of thousands of yellow plastic ducks, the kind you give to little children to play with when they have a bath. It was – it seemed – an ordinary shipping accident, to be filed away in the insurance company's records.

The ducks did not agree. They spread through the oceans, letting themselves be pushed cheerfully by the wind, the waves, the currents, letting themselves be washed up on the beaches of the world and making it possible for oceanographers to understand many things about the workings of the oceans and the currents.

The image of the intrepid, smiling little ducks on the crests of gigantic waves in a stormy ocean filled Roberto with an absurd, incredible, invincible joy. He thought of the current that had brought him to this beach after a long stormy voyage, and it seemed to him, now that he was here, that there was only one thing he had to do. Just one.

It was then that he entered the water.

They were fine waves, he thought, paddling out with his hands off the sides of the board. Considering how far from any ocean they were, they weren't bad at all. At least five feet, maybe even slightly more. He let the first one pass underneath him, without even trying to stand. He felt a calm sensation of inevitability. The kind that lets you delay things as long as you want without any fear or anxiety.

He let the second wave go by, and then he saw a bigger one forming, more than seven feet high. The one he'd come here for.

He stiffened his arms and gripped the front of the board, pushed the tips of his toes onto the back and stayed like that, still. As if everything around him had become motionless and eternal.

Then eternity ended.

He stretched his arms, grabbed the rails of the board, contracted his abdominal muscles, and swung himself up. His knees were probably hurting, but he did not notice. He got up into a standing position and the board shot forward.

If he had already read then the books he would read later, Roberto would have been able to describe the sensation he felt, once again riding the wave, as if he had never stopped, not even for one day.

He would have been able to say that it was an intoxication that cut everything straight down the middle: time, space, sadness, good and evil, love and pain and joy and guilt. And forgiveness – even the most difficult kind, the kind we ask of ourselves. And the circle of life, and the stories of fathers and sons and their desperate search for each other.

INVOLUNTARY WITNESS

Gianrico Carofiglio

A nine-year-old boy is found murdered at the bottom of a well near a popular beach resort in southern Italy. In what looks like a hopeless case for Guido Guerrieri, counsel for the defence, a Senegalese peddler is accused of the crime. Faced with small-town racism fuelled by the recent immigration from Africa, Guido attempts to exploit the esoteric workings of the Italian courts.

More than a perfectly paced legal thriller, this relentless suspense novel transcends the genre. A powerful attack on racism, and a fascinating insight into the Italian judicial process, it is also an affectionate portrait of a deeply humane hero.

PRAISE FOR *INVOLUNTARY WITNESS*

"A stunner. Guerrieri is a wonderfully convincing character; morose, but seeing the absurdity of his gloomy life, his vulnerability and cynicism laced with self-deprecating humour. It is the veracity of the setting and the humanity of the lawyer that makes the novel a courtroom drama of such rare quality."
The Times

"Involuntary Witness raises the standard for crime fiction. Carofiglio's deft touch has given us a story that is both literary and gritty – and one that speeds along like the best legal thrillers. His insights into human nature – good and bad – are breathtaking." *Jeffery Deaver*

"A powerful redemptive novel beautifully translated."
Daily Mail

www.bitterlemonpress.com

A WALK IN THE DARK

Gianrico Carofiglio

When Martina accuses her ex-boyfriend – the son of a powerful local judge – of assault and battery, no witnesses can be persuaded to testify on her behalf, and one lawyer after another refuses to represent her. Guido Guerrieri knows the case could bring his legal career to a premature and messy end, but he cannot resist the appeal of a hopeless cause. Nor deny an attraction to Sister Claudia, the young woman in charge of the shelter where Martina is living, who shares his love of martial arts and his virulent hatred of injustice.

A Walk in the Dark, Carofiglio's second novel featuring defence counsel Guerrieri, follows on from the critical and commercial success of *Involuntary Witness*.

PRAISE FOR *A WALK IN THE DARK*

"Carofiglio is a prosecutor well known for his courageous anti-mafia stance, which has attracted death threats. *A Walk in the Dark* features an engagingly complex, emotional and moody defence lawyer, Guido Guerrieri, who takes on cases shunned by his colleagues. In passing, Carofiglio provides a fascinating insight into the workings of the Italian criminal justice system." *Observer*

"Part legal thriller, part insight into a man fighting his own demons. Every character in Carofiglio's fiction has a story to tell and they are always worth hearing. As the author himself is an anti-mafia prosecutor, this powerfully affecting novel benefits from veracity as well as tight writing." *The Daily Mail*

"At one level an exciting courtroom thriller, but what places it in a superior league is the portrayal of a slice of Italian society not normally encountered in crime fiction and an immensely appealing flawed hero." *The Times*

www.bitterlemonpress.com

REASONABLE DOUBTS

Gianrico Carofiglio

Counsel for the defence Guido Guerrieri is asked to handle the appeal of Fabio Paolicelli, who has been sentenced to sixteen years for drug smuggling. The odds are stacked against the accused: not only the fact that he initially confessed to the crime, but also his past as a neo-Fascist thug. It is only the intervention of Paolicelli's beautiful half-Japanese wife that finally overcomes Guerrieri's reluctance.

Reasonable Doubts, Carofiglio's third novel featuring Guerrieri, follows on from the critical and commercial success of *Involuntary Witness* and *A Walk in the Dark*.

PRAISE FOR *REASONABLE DOUBTS*

"The role of lawyer Guido Guerrieri is to take on impossible cases that have little chance of success. The lawyer accepts this case only because he's fallen in lust with the prisoner's wife; his efforts to prove his client's innocence bring him into dangerous conflict with Mafia interests. Everything a legal thriller should be." *The Times*

This novel is hard-boiled and sun-dried in equal parts. Guerrieri stumbles into a case involving old enmities, a femme fatale and a murky conspiracy. But where Philip Marlowe would be knocking back bourbon and listening to the snap of fist on jaw, Guerrieri prefers Sicilian wine and Leonard Cohen... The local colour is complemented by snappy legal procedural writing which sends the reader tumbling through the clockwork of a tightly wound plot." *The Financial Times*

"Carofiglio, until recently an anti-Mafia prosecutor in southern Italy, is particularly well placed to write legal thrillers, and he does so with considerable brio, humour and skill." *The Daily Mail*

www.bitterlemonpress.com

TEMPORARY PERFECTIONS

Gianrico Carofiglio

It all began with an unusual assignment, a job better suited for Marlowe than for defence counsel Guido Guerrieri. Could he find new evidence to force the police to reopen their investigation of the disappearance of Manuela, the daughter of a rich couple living in Bari? The stories of Manuela's druggy university friends don't quite add up. Her best friend, Caterina, too beautiful and certainly too young for Guerrieri, is a temptation he doesn't need.

He fights his loneliness by talking to the punching bag hanging in his living room and by walking the streets of Bari late at night, activities that somehow lead to solving the riddle of Manuela's vanishing.

PRAISE FOR *TEMPORARY PERFECTIONS*

"This is not only a fascinating panorama of Bari's neon-lit underworld. It's a fine literary achievement: a study of angst and the efforts of a disillusioned hero to find some integrity in a shady world."
Independent

"The novel has a wider canvas than most novels of this type and the sprightly writing, as well as the twists and turns of the plot, ensure that interest never flags." *Times Literary Supplement*

"Carofiglio's legal thrillers (this is the fourth), stand out for me as being among the very best of the slew of European crime books to hit our shelves, which perhaps isn't surprising when one learns the author was an anti-Mafia prosecutor before becoming a member of the Italian Senate." *Daily Mail*

"Guido Guerrieri has become one of crime fiction's most endearing characters. The first-person narrative by the insecure and self-deprecating lawyer teems with wit and provides a perceptive commentary on Italian life, law and mores." *The Times*

www.bitterlemonpress.com